The COLOR
of
LOVE

By
Julianne MacLean

Prologue

⸒ᴄ꙰ꙷ꙰ᴄꙷꙷ⸓

How powerful is love, exactly? Is it strong enough to ward off death? And if so, where does that sort of warrior love come from? Who creates it or sends it to you when you're shivering in a cold dark cave, alone and without hope? Is it God? Or are we, each of us, on our own, responsible for the love that grows and lives in our hearts?

By all accounts, I should be a dead man. It's a miracle I'm alive today to tell this story, which brings me back to my initial question: Does love have the power to thrust a person into danger, test his fortitude, push him to the brink of madness, all for the sole purpose of leading him to the place he's meant to be? Or is it all just luck and coincidence?

I still don't know the answers to those questions, and I have no idea why certain events in my life transpired as they did. All I know is that the result was extraordinary and astounds me to this day.

What is so special about me? Who am I?

I am just a man—a man who was saved by love.

Choices

Adapted from the journal of Seth Jameson

I'm not sure where to begin, so I guess I'll start by thanking God that I brought this empty notebook on the plane. I'm not much of a writer but clearly there's a story here to tell, so I'll do my best to document everything that has happened so far.

I only hope I don't run out of paper or ink before we're rescued.

If we're rescued.

It's been four days and we haven't seen a single sign of anything resembling a search.

But let me go back first, and explain how I got here.

It all began two weeks ago when I received a phone call from Mike Lawson, one of my climbing buddies from Australia. Mike and I had grown up together and we met in Nepal fifteen years ago on our first Everest expedition, and reached the summit together in a perfect moment of triumph and exhaustion.

I was only twenty-one at the time (Mike was twenty-four) and I've since reached the summit six times. Not on my own, of course. I've been working as a team leader and guide, helping others travel up the mountain from base camp to achieve their dreams. Mike has remained a close friend and twice he has joined me to help guide others to the top of the world.

Outside of that, we spend a good deal of time apart, pursuing our own personal ambitions, climbing mountains all over the world and always seeking out media opportunities that could lead to sponsorships, with the goal to find a way to feed our alpine addictions.

As I write these words—while contemplating the unbelievable situation I find myself in—I can't possibly deny the truth of that statement. That my desire to scale mountains is exactly that: an addiction I have never been able to control.

Just like alcohol or cocaine, the craving to propel myself to new and different peaks each year holds me in its grip, causing me to ignore and lose sight of the people who matter most in my life, while I selfishly feed the beast inside me.

Two weeks ago, Mike called me at my cabin in Maine to discuss a mountaineering prospect in Iceland. Because we keep in touch regularly through social media, I already knew Mike had been hired by George Atherton, a billionaire philanthropist, to lead a group of climbers to the top of the Eyjafjallajökull volcano.

It's an easy one-day hike over snow and ice, but what interested me most about the expedition was the fact that a camera crew would be tagging along to film a documentary about the billionaire who was funding the trip.

Mike had intended to lead the hike with his current climbing partner and significant other, Julie Peters, but Julie broke her ankle while skiing in Quebec a week before shooting was scheduled to begin. Mike wanted me to drop everything and fly to Iceland to take her place.

Since I'd been dealing with my Everest clients through email (that expedition will occur in March, April and May), I didn't see why I couldn't continue to manage that from Iceland and make a few extra bucks in the process. The film shoot was supposed to be a quick three-day gig, after all, and who knew what might come of it? Mike and I both want to make names for ourselves in the climbing world, and judging by the filmmakers who are on board for the project, it's quite possible that the doc could win some awards.

Naturally, I said yes and hopped a flight to Halifax, Nova Scotia, where I connected with some members of the film crew. We then flew directly to Reykjavik on Mr. Atherton's private corporate jet.

It was a decision I now wish I could reverse.

Everything seemed normal during takeoff. Though perhaps "normal" isn't the right word to describe the flight, for there I sat—Mr. Cheapskate Economy Class—in a soft and spacious mocha-colored swiveling leather chair. I was unshaven with a slouchy ribbed woolen toque on my head, my backpack at my feet, enjoying fifty-year-old single malt scotch on the rocks in a sparkling crystal tumbler. I don't want to overdo it, but just before takeoff, the producer handed me a box of assorted Swiss chocolates. I opened it and helped myself.

I'd never flown in such luxury before and couldn't believe my good luck. *How did I get here?* I wondered.

There were only three of us on board—not including the two pilots—but none of us had met before.

The guy beside me who'd handed me the chocolates was one of the producers of the documentary. His name was Jason Mehta and he told me he was nervous about the climb because he wasn't much of an outdoorsman. The most strenuous thing he ever did was run on a treadmill at the city gym.

I assured him he had nothing to worry about because it was more of a "hike" than an actual "climb."

(Secretly—because I'd already summited Everest five times—I felt it was beneath me to lead climbers on such an easy excursion, but I didn't express that to anyone, least of all Mike.)

The guy across from me in the facing seat was a cameraman, and he was mostly concerned about his equipment and how the batteries were going to hold up in the cold temperatures at high altitudes.

He told me his name was Aaron and he was from Boston.

"I'm Seth," I said, leaning forward to shake his hand. "Good to meet you."

He fell asleep not long after takeoff, so we didn't speak again until much later.

I still don't know what went wrong. Neither of us do. All we remember is waking up to some wicked turbulence somewhere over the Atlantic.

"What the hell?" I groaned, waking from a nap and sitting up in my seat to look out the window.

Beyond the glass, it was pitch black except for the flashing navigation lights on the wingtip of the aircraft, which sent an eerie glow into the clouds.

Bang! Crash! The plane thumped up and down.

I'd never experienced such a deafening clamor on a jet before, and it caused my insides to wrench into a tight knot. I gripped the armrests with both hands and met Aaron's gaze across from me. He must have woken up around the same time I did.

"Geez," he said, his body pressed stiffly against the seat back. "They need to get us out of here."

"No kidding," Jason agreed.

Bump! Thwack! A warning bell pinged repeatedly.

The three of us fell silent while the plane shuddered and thrashed about in the sky, pitching and rolling in a sickening sequence of side-to-side figure eights.

At last the plane leveled out, but it continued to slam up and down on giant boulder-like pockets of air.

I'd never felt such fear. All I could do was clench my jaw, grip the armrests and squeeze my eyes shut while I prayed for everything to be over.

Then suddenly the nose of the plane dipped sharply and we plunged forward into a rapid, spiraling descent. Jason began screaming in terror, but I could utter no sounds. My chest and lungs constricted; my vocal chords wouldn't work.

My mind was screaming, however. Dreadful thoughts were banging around inside my head.

I didn't want to die. I wanted to live and fix the things I'd done wrong.

Please God, make it stop. I just want one more chance. If you let me live, I'll do better. I'll be a better father. I won't break any more promises.

But God couldn't have been listening, because we continued to dive toward the earth while the hellish terror raged on.

At no point did the pilots say anything to us on the intercom. Looking back on it, I suppose they were too busy fighting with the controls, trying to save our lives.

In those final moments, I opened my eyes and turned my head toward the window. There was nothing out there but blackness, interrupted only by the rapid flashing of the wing light on the mist.

⌒⌒⌒

As we were going down, I was certain we were all going to die. I believed it because I assumed we were crashing into the ice-filled waters of the North Atlantic.

I wish I could describe all the details of the crash, but it happened so fast I could barely make sense of it. All I remember is the motion of the plane as the engine roared, then the nose pointed upward ever so slightly, and I felt a strong, sudden lift beneath us, as if we were taking off again.

The sensation gave me hope. Was it possible the pilots had regained control? But the very next instant, we were jolted in our seats as the wing of the plane collided with something and broke away. The deafening sound of steel ripping apart and glass shattering overwhelmed my ability to think. Somehow, through my debilitating panic, I managed to turn my head and saw a gaping hole in the side the plane.

The seat Jason had occupied only seconds ago was gone and that part of the floor was missing.

A fierce ice-cold wind gusted through the interior of the cabin as we scraped at full speed over jagged treetops. Evergreen branches and trunks splintered and exploded as we careened through woods, and I felt as if my insides were going to burst into flame from the sheer fright of it all.

I don't know what finally stopped us. I must have blacked out for those final seconds because when I opened my eyes and sucked in a breath, everything was dark and quiet.

Was I blind? Or dead?

The whole world seemed to have gone pitch black. There were no cabin lights, no sounds of movement or voices.

Only then, when the freezing air entered my throat, did I know I was alive.

Feeling suddenly trapped, I thrashed about in my seat and struggled to unbuckle myself, but my hands shook uncontrollably. I could barely get a grip on anything.

When at last I was free, I leaned forward to squint through the darkness at Aaron, the cameraman from Boston, who was seated across from me. All I could decipher was the shadow of his immobile form. Was he alive? I had no idea.

"Aaron," I managed to mutter. "Are you all right?"

He gave no reply.

Then I remembered my cell phone in the pocket of my vest. I'd turned it off just before takeoff, but it was fully charged.

Quickly withdrawing it, I pushed the power button and waited for the screen to light up.

The familiar musical sound of the device filled me with relief, and I waited for it to find a signal so I could dial 911.

But there was no service. "Damn it," I whispered, then leaned forward in my seat to shine the glow of the screen upon Aaron.

He was hunched over sideways. His whole face was drenched in blood.

"Oh God," I whispered. Moving closer to try and help him, I took hold of his wrist and found a pulse, then shone my cell phone light over the top of his head to search for the source of the bleeding.

It appeared to be a clean gash just above his hairline, but not life threatening, as long as his skull wasn't fractured. He must have been sliced by a flying piece of metal or some other loose object.

"Aaron," I said, shaking his shoulder. "Can you hear me?"

Still, he offered no response, so I applied pressure to the wound for a moment while I tried to figure out what to do next.

Rising from my seat, I searched for my backpack and found it shoved up against the bulkhead. Quickly I rifled through it for my flashlight, knife, and first aid kit, then returned to help him.

Within minutes I had wrapped a bandage around his head and was on my feet, checking my cell phone for service again.

Still nothing, and I'd spent enough time in remote locations to know that if I let the phone continue to search for a signal, the battery would be dead within an hour. So I shut it down to conserve the battery, slipped it into my back pocket and shone my flashlight around what was left of the interior of the plane.

For a somber moment, I paused to stare at the place where Jason had been sitting not long ago. How lucky for me that I had chosen my seat and not his when we boarded.

Poor Jason. I wondered if he was alive out there somewhere…

Beneath the hole in the floor was a bed of snow, and along the open side, a thick wall of evergreen boughs.

Carefully, I turned and made my way toward the flight deck to check on the pilots.

To get there, I had to step over my large backpack and a mess of dented aluminum crates that must have flown forward from the galley.

I found the cockpit door unlocked, but I struggled to open it because the panel was warped and had become wedged against the floor.

When I finally squeezed through the narrow opening and shone my light on the scene, it was not what I'd hoped to find.

The nose section of the jet had been completely smashed in. Thick spruce branches filled what was left of the space. I wrestled with the prickly growth, fighting to thrust the disorderly green boughs out of the way, but in the end, all I found were two dead pilots, their bodies crushed between the flight control panel and bulkhead.

The gruesome sight of their lifeless eyes caused me to lose my breath, and I stumbled back, fell out of the cockpit and landed on my back on top of the cabin debris.

Panic and nausea flooded through me. I slammed the door shut with my boot.

That's when I heard the scream.

୧ℂ᠔ᠥ

It's okay, it's okay!" I shouted as I scrambled to my feet and hurried to Aaron's side.

He was thrashing about in his seat like a chained-up animal.

"We're okay!" I assured him. "The plane crashed, but we're fine."

He fumbled clumsily with the seatbelt buckle. "Get me out of here."

"It's easy. Look…There." I flicked the mechanism and freed him.

Aaron leapt out of his seat and tripped over my backpack.

"Where are we?" he asked, his eyes darting about.

"We're inside the plane," I explained. "We crashed into some trees, but I don't know anything more than that."

He took a moment to gather his wits. "Are we in Iceland?" he asked.

I was relieved that he was at least conscious of where we'd been heading. I was worried for a few seconds that because of his head wound he might not remember anything.

"I don't think so," I replied. "Based on when we left Halifax, we're probably in Newfoundland. I thought we were over the water when we were going down, but clearly we weren't, which was damn lucky for us. Or maybe it wasn't luck. Maybe the pilots had intentionally flown us to dry land."

Aaron wobbled and staggered sideways, then reached for the back of a seat to steady himself.

"Sit down." I reached out to help him. "You were hit on the head."

"Shit," he said.

"Don't worry. It's a clean wound and I stopped the bleeding, but you might have a mild concussion. I don't know. I'm not a doctor."

Aaron sat still for a moment, staring straight ahead. "Where's Jason?" he asked.

I hesitated, then shook my head. "The wing of the plane was ripped off when we were landing. He must have been sucked out. It's possible he might be alive somewhere, if we weren't too far off the ground when he fell. He was buckled into his seat, so the cushions might have provided some padding."

"Should we go look for him?" Aaron asked.

Again I shook my head. "It's too dark. We'll wait until morning, and even then, we shouldn't stray too far because the search planes will be looking for the wreckage. We'll need to be ready to signal them."

"You think they'll come in the morning?" Aaron asked.

"Of course, if not before then," I replied. "This jet belongs to a billionaire. I'm sure he'll be missing it, and the pilots must have radioed that we were in trouble."

Aaron slouched back in the seat and closed his eyes. "What about the pilots?"

"Both dead," I told him without elaborating. "And there's no power and the nose is completely crushed, so I don't think there's any hope of using the radio. I tried my cell phone but couldn't get a signal."

"What about GPS so we know where we are?"

I shook my head. "Without a mobile network, my phone will be dead within an hour just trying to find a signal. I'm keeping it shut off for now."

Neither of us said anything for a long time, then Aaron began to shiver. "It's freezing in here."

Maybe it was adrenaline, but I'd barely noticed the cold until he mentioned it. Then I realized my extremities were growing numb.

Geez. I was a seasoned climber and wasn't proud of the fact that I hadn't been more on top of this. I blamed it on the shock of the crash.

"You're right," I said. "We need to keep warm and make it through the night without freezing. That's the most important thing. Help me get some stuff out of my pack."

Five

⸙

We barely slept a wink that night.

Because I had only one sleeping bag and we couldn't find Aaron's jacket (it must have blown out of the plane when the wing broke off, along with his cell phone which was in the pocket), we had to share what I had in my pack. This included an insulated parka I'd brought in addition to the jacket I was wearing.

We didn't talk much. What exactly do you chat about with a total stranger when you're shivering in the cold and weighing the fact that you just survived a plane crash, when others didn't? And two of those lost souls were only a few feet away, so it seemed proper, somehow, to remain silent.

When the sun finally came up, I nudged Aaron, tossed off the sleeping bag, and rose stiffly. My body felt sluggish and heavy from the cold, but my hands and feet were okay. I told Aaron to keep checking his extremities and not to ignore any numbness, then I crossed to the hole in the side of the plane to examine the situation in the light of day.

"We need to get out of here and see where we are," I said, "and make sure the wreckage is visible from the sky."

With the daylight, it was easier to establish what we were dealing with, at least in terms of an exit strategy. I made sure my gloves were on tight, then attempted to push some of the prickly branches out of the way. I discovered we were wedged tightly up against a giant black spruce.

"We won't be leaving through here," I said, giving up the task.

"Let's try the door," Aaron suggested.

Together we managed to open the passenger door which included an integral set of steps. I descended first and hopped into a foot and a half of snow.

"You stay where you are for now," I said to Aaron who stood on the steps. "It's important to stay dry."

There was not a single breath of wind in the air as I waded through the snow to gain some distance from the plane and get a better view of the wreckage.

"*Jesus...*" I whispered as I took in the devastated nose section and strips of steel ripped like thin ribbons from the length of the fuselage. The tail end was in shreds too. It was a miracle Aaron and I had survived.

"It doesn't help that the plane is white," I said to him. "The trees are tall and covered in snow. The branches are hiding most of the wreckage. Let's hope we left an obvious trail of damage when we were landing."

A snowflake fell on my nose just then. I looked up through a hole in the trees at the cloudy sky. *Great...Just what we need.*

"They should know where we are, though, shouldn't they?" Aaron asked. "I mean...the pilots must have radioed that we were in trouble."

"Of course," I replied, wading back to the plane. "But still, we should do something to make it easier for them to spot us. I have a red tent in my backpack. We'll find the nearest clearing and fly it like a flag. And we should keep busy today in case they don't find us right away. We'll need to light a fire to keep warm and then take stock of what we have for supplies."

I returned to the steps and glanced briefly at the pilots' frozen remains, visible through the smashed-in window as I climbed back up.

Again, I thought about what had been on my mind as the plane was zigzagging through the turbulence and I believed we were plunging to our deaths.

Carla and Kaleigh.

The snow began to fall lightly around 9:00 a.m., and by noon Aaron and I were huddled inside the plane, grateful to have a roof over our heads while a vicious blizzard raged outside.

I didn't bother to find a place to lay out my tent as a distress signal because it would have been buried within an hour. Either that, or it would have been ripped away by the wind.

And we couldn't venture out to search for Jason.

All we could do was sit and wait out the storm, uncomfortably aware that any potential search and rescue attempts would also have to be postponed until the weather cleared.

"I guess it's lucky for me that you're a mountaineer," Aaron said as he rubbed his palms together over the small fire I'd lit on an aluminum tray inside the plane. "I can honestly say, no one else I know would pull an ice ax, ropes and a thermal sleeping bag out of his carry-on."

I leaned back in my seat and regarded Aaron curiously. "I have two axes. One for each hand. But you must know something about climbing if they hired you to film us going up the side of the volcano."

He chuckled. "No, I'm a city boy through and through. This isn't even my day job. I'm just here because I own a decent high def camera and a Go Pro."

"You're kidding me." My eyebrows pulled together in surprise. "So you don't know anything about climbing?"

"Not a thing." He raised his boot to show me. "I just bought these hiking boots two days ago, and I got the Go Pro because I wanted to film tropical fish when I went snorkeling in Mexico last year."

"What's your day job, then?" I asked, intrigued but unimpressed.

"I'm a therapist, and I teach guitar lessons on the side."

"How do you know George Atherton?"

Aaron continued to hold his hands over the fire. "He's a client."

Maybe it was bad manners, but I laughed. "So are you his therapist or his guitar teacher?"

"Therapist. But don't worry, he hired an experienced D.O.P. to be in charge of the shoot, and from what I hear, the guy's a real pro." Aaron leaned to the side and gestured toward his camera case at the front of the plane. "I doubt I'll be shooting anything now. My camera's probably wrecked."

"Cameras can be replaced," I carefully reminded him.

Aaron's gaze met mine. "Yeah. We were lucky last night."

While we considered the loss of life and pondered the miracle of our existence on that day, the wind howled like a beast through the treetops overhead. Then suddenly...*boom*! There was a thunderous explosion and the whole plane shook.

Aaron jolted and looked up. "What was that?"

I remained seated in a lazy sprawl, slightly amused as I peered up at him. "Relax city boy. A big clump of snow just slid off a tree and landed on the roof."

He let out a breath and relaxed. "Ah." Then he frowned. "No chance we'll get buried alive in here…"

"Don't worry," I replied. "I'm keeping a close eye on the situation."

"Good to know," he said uneasily.

As I watched him lay another stick on the fire, I wondered if I should search for that bottle of single malt scotch, because the poor guy was seriously out of his element. He could probably have used a drink or two right then.

I could have used a couple myself.

News

CHAPTER

Seven

❧

Carla Matthews
Boston, Massachusetts

I was in the kitchen cooking cheesy bowtie pasta for Kaleigh when the telephone rang. She had just arrived home from school and was doing her homework on the sofa.

"Hello," I said, resting the receiver on my shoulder as I strained the pasta over the sink.

The voice on the other end caught me by surprise. I immediately set down the colander and turned to face Kaleigh, who was punching numbers into her calculator and scribbling in her notebook.

"Hi Gladys," I said. "It's nice to hear from you. It's been a while."

Over a year, in fact.

Not that I was counting the days or anything.

But *seriously*. One would think a sixty-year-old woman living alone would take more interest in seeing her only grandchild.

Like mother like son, I supposed.

"What's going on?" I asked.

She breathed heavily into the mouthpiece and let out a tiny whimper.

With growing concern, I faced the sink again. "What's wrong? Are you all right?"

"I'm fine," she replied at last, "but something's happened to Seth. Have you been watching the news?"

"No," I replied. "What is it? Was he climbing?"

Did he fall? Was it altitude sickness again?

I'd been preparing myself for this phone call since the first time he left me, eleven years ago.

Heart racing, I waited for Gladys to go on.

"He was on his way to Iceland to be in a movie about that billionaire, George Atherton, but they lost track of the plane. They think they crashed somewhere up north, probably over the Atlantic. I can't believe it."

She began to sob into the phone while I strove to comprehend what I was hearing. I couldn't believe it either. *A plane crash?* Surely there had to be some mistake.

"How many people were on board?" I asked.

"It was just a small private jet so there were only three passengers, plus two pilots. I didn't even know he was going to Iceland. He didn't mention it to me. Did he tell *you?*"

I cupped my forehead in my hand while a wave of nausea crashed over me. "No. The last time we spoke was Christmas Day and he didn't say anything about it. He called from out west, somewhere in the Rockies. Other than that, it's been over a year since we've seen him."

"I'm sorry," she said. "I'm always telling him to go home and be with the two of you, but he never listens. That boy…He was always such a free spirit."

Free spirit…?

How about commitment-phobe?

I exhaled and tried not to think negative thoughts, not at a time like this. "Are they sure the plane actually went down? Is there any chance they just lost contact with it?"

I didn't want to give up hope. Not yet.

"They interviewed Atherton on the news a few minutes ago," Gladys told me. "He's very concerned because the pilots sounded distressed when they last heard from them. They were heading into a storm and wanted to change course, but then they lost contact completely. It was like the plane just disappeared into thin air."

My stomach turned over again. "Oh, God, I can't believe this. Have they started searching yet?"

"Yes, but they don't even know if they're looking in the right place, and now they're saying there are blizzards in the area so they might have to hold off. But if the plane did change course, it could have crashed anywhere. From what I understand, they're searching the waters north of Newfoundland, looking for some sign of the wreckage."

Wreckage. The word turned me into a big puddle of grief. I couldn't bear to think about Seth being on that plane when it was careening from the sky, and how terrifying that must have been.

"This is a nightmare," I said shakily. "What am I going to tell Kaleigh?"

"I don't know," Gladys replied. "But let's not lose hope. I can't accept that he's gone. Not my boy. I have to believe he's still alive out there somewhere."

I nodded and wiped a tear from my eye. "I'll keep my hopes up too, Gladys," I replied, "and I'll say lots of prayers. Keep me posted if you hear anything. And I'll do the same."

We hung up and I took a moment to gather my composure before I went into the living room to tell my daughter that her father's plane had gone missing.

CHAPTER

Eight

⌐cᗡ᙭ᓝᑐ

That night I climbed into bed beside Kaleigh to read to her, but it wasn't easy to focus on the adventures of a vampire bunny while I was waiting fretfully for news about Seth's plane. Nevertheless I carried on and tried not to behave in a way that might upset her before bed.

When we came to the end of the chapter, I closed the book and kissed the top of her head. "Time to go to sleep now. We'll read more tomorrow."

I was about to slip out of her room and return to the computer to check for news about Seth when she called out to me.

"Mom?"

I paused in the doorway and turned around. "Yes?"

Her forehead was crinkled in that familiar way that caused my heart to throb. Kaleigh had always struggled with sleep issues. I suspected it was going to be a long night.

"I feel bad," she said.

Slowly I returned to her side and sat on the edge of the bed. "Because of what's happening with your dad?"

"Sort of."

I stroked her dark hair away from her face. "I feel scared too, honey, but I'm trying not to lose hope. Maybe the plane landed somewhere different, that's all."

She continued to peer up at me with those anxious eyes. "That's not what I feel bad about," she explained. "I feel bad because…"

"Why?" I gently asked. "You can tell me."

She hesitated, then finally admitted the truth. "Because I'm not very upset."

Her words hit me like a punch in the gut, but I worked hard to hide it. "What do you mean?"

Kaleigh shrugged. "I know he's my dad and everything, but I'm not worried like you are. I don't feel like crying, and that makes me think I'm a bad person."

At last I understood, and I couldn't blame her for how she was feeling. She was only eleven years old and Seth hadn't been around much. She barely knew him.

"You're not a bad person," I insisted. "And you're right, you don't know him very well, and that's not your fault. He travels a lot and you've never had the chance. But I do know that he loves you in his own way."

"How do you know that?" she asked. "Did he tell you?"

This was torture. I didn't know how to answer her question, so I did what any good mother would do. I lied.

"Of course he told me. He tells me all the time, and don't ever think otherwise. The reason he couldn't live with us is because…" I paused. "He was always…" I wasn't sure how to phrase it. Then finally I found the right words.

"Your dad is a free spirit," I told her. "He has a passion for climbing big mountains and that has nothing to do with us. That's just the way he's built. He can't stay put in one place for very long."

"Then why did you marry him?" she asked, point-blank, and I felt my head draw back slightly.

These were not easy questions. I'm not even sure I knew the answer to this particular one myself.

"Because I was in love," I finally said, "and I wanted you to have a father."

She stared at me with a look of bewilderment. "But I *don't* have a father," she said. "Not like my friends do. They have dads who come to their dance recitals and help them with their homework."

Swallowing uneasily, I leaned forward and kissed her on the forehead. "I'm sorry about that, Kaleigh. Please believe me when I say that I always wanted that for you. I thought that if your dad and I got married, he might stick around and do all of those things, but it just didn't happen that way."

My relationship with Seth had always been complicated, and to this day I wonder why I clung so tightly to the hope that he might eventually change and become the man I wanted him to be.

We'd been dating only briefly when I got pregnant with Kaleigh. Not long after I told him about it—I was only two months along at the time—he received a phone call from a buddy in Australia and high-tailed it out of town before I reached my third trimester.

Off he went to climb Everest again, explaining that it was the opportunity of a lifetime, that he would be leading a prestigious team of climbers to the summit for a whopping paycheck that would solve all our money problems and give Kaleigh the life she deserved. He'd said he wanted to marry me. We would tie the knot when he came home.

Of course I let him go. I never wanted to be a ball and chain to *any* man.

He sent money when he could, but otherwise I didn't hear from him for weeks on end, then weeks stretched into months, and I had no choice but to figure out how to survive on my own. He didn't even make it home for Kaleigh's birth.

Whenever I asked Seth when he'd be coming home, there were always excuses—like he had another climb coming up and he had to train, or he was traveling Down Under to scope out new trails across the Outback for novice adventurers. There were always paychecks of course, and he promised to send money home. Sometimes he did, sometimes he didn't.

It wasn't long after Kaleigh was weaned from the bottle that I accepted I'd be raising her alone, and for a few years, I did exactly that.

Then we received a phone call.

He was coming home at last—after a disastrous climb up K2 in Pakistan where he'd suffered severe altitude sickness. His climbing partners had to drag him, barely conscious, down the mountain on a makeshift stretcher with ropes. They never did reach the summit.

He said that was the climb that made him question his decision to live such a roving lifestyle, one without commitment to anything outside of the next peak. He wept on the phone and begged me for a second chance. He promised he was a changed man and knew what was important now. He told me he wanted to get married, and the sooner the better.

On the day we greeted him at the airport, I was hesitant. Cautiously hopeful, at best. But when he scooped Kaleigh up in his arms, held her against him, and kissed the top of her head, I knew something was different. He gazed at me with tears in his eyes. He looked so gaunt.

What can I say? I melted. And I forgave everything.

I truly believed he was home for good that time.

―ₒ

I don't know what it was about Seth Jameson, but sometimes he had a way of breaking down my defenses and making me forget all the false promises, and all the times he'd walked out on me.

On top of that, I'd been struggling as a single mom—both financially and emotionally—and let's face it, I was lonely. I wanted a family, and I believed, after that close brush with death, that Seth had finally changed his priorities and valued the same things I did.

I was wrong. Six months after we signed the marriage certificate at city hall, he was gone again. Just like that. Back to the Himalayas...

The phone rang suddenly, and I sat up on Kaleigh's bed. Glancing down at her with weary eyes, I realized that she was asleep. I must have drifted off as well.

The phone rang a second time so I hurried out of her room to answer it.

Please, God. Let it be good news...

Storms

CHAPTER

Nine

Adapted from the journal of Seth Jameson

The blizzard raged on throughout the day and didn't let up until after midnight. By then the temperature had plummeted to dangerously below freezing and Aaron and I had no choice but to remain inside the aircraft.

We were lucky in that we found one of the pilot's winter jackets balled up in an overhead luggage compartment. I handed it to Aaron to claim as his own.

The following morning the storm cleared and the sun shone brightly, but we had some trouble opening the door and lowering the steps because of the monstrous drifts that had blown in and surrounded the plane during the night.

When we finally forced the door open, it became clear there was no way we could travel anywhere in fresh snow of that depth, so I tore four aluminum panels from the galley area, lashed them to our boots and fashioned two pairs of practical snowshoes.

Bundled up for the weather, I grabbed the red tent in my pack and we ventured outside to search for a large enough area to lay out a visible signal or perhaps tie it to a tree top.

The first thing I did was locate my compass and scan the area for landmarks.

"Are you afraid we'll get lost?" Aaron asked.

"Not if I take a bearing." My eyes lifted. "Do you know how to read a compass?"

He shook his head. "No. City boy, remember?"

"Come here, then," I said. "You should learn." I held the instrument up so he could see it.

All at once I felt a pang of regret as I remembered that this compass had been a gift from Carla. She'd given it to me for my birthday the year after Kaleigh was born and she'd had something inscribed on the back.

I didn't have to withdraw it from the leather case to remember what it said. The words were imprinted on my brain, because on so many occasions, they'd weighed on me like a piano on my back.

So you'll always find your way home. Love Carla

I swallowed uneasily as I remembered the promise I'd made on the plane. *Had God actually been listening?* Perhaps not.

Steadying myself in the snow, I focused on the task of teaching Aaron how *not* to get lost.

"The first thing you need to do is establish a field bearing so we can navigate in a straight line. See here…This is the direction-of-travel arrow, and we're going to backtrack that way." I pointed. "In the direction the plane came down."

"Why that direction?" he asked.

"Because we probably cleared out some trees," I replied. "It makes sense to signal from there."

"All right. Maybe we'll find Jason," Aaron added.

Probably not alive, I thought.

Choosing to keep that to myself, I continued the compass lesson. "Next we rotate the housing until the red end of the needle is centered above the orienteering needle. Now take this reading here, and this is our bearing. We'll pick out some landmarks along this route and keep track so we'll be able to find our way back to the plane."

"Sounds simple enough," Aaron said.

I wish I could say it was, but we barely made it fifty feet before I had to make a radical change to our plan.

A t first, when I spotted the wide clearing just ahead, beyond a cluster of snow-covered balsam firs, I thought we'd finally gotten a lucky break.

I should have known it was never wise to make assumptions in the wild.

"Shit," I said, lifting my snow goggles to look up the side of the mountain.

"What is it?" Aaron pushed through some snow-covered trees and caught up to me.

"This isn't good," I replied.

"Why?"

"*Be quiet.*" I held up a hand and listened to the silence of the forest. Then—*very gently*—I stomped my foot on the snow and took note of the sound it made.

How long had it been since the storm ended?

About eight hours.

"What's going on?" Aaron whispered.

I continued to scan the area all around us, then pointed my gloved hand at the slopes to our left and to our right. In a low voice I explained, "We're in a valley here, and we couldn't be in a worse position because this isn't just a clearing. It's an avalanche debris field. Look, see?" I pointed at some broken trees and blocks of ice on both sides. "We can't stay here."

"Should we go back to the plane?" Aaron asked.

I turned in the direction we had come. "Just to get what we need. There was a ton of snow last night. If there's a slide, the plane will get buried with us inside it. We have to find a safe route to move up the ridge. That might put us in a better location to be spotted by rescue planes anyway."

Aaron looked up. "It looks pretty steep."

"It's not that bad," I assured him. "Probably only a 40 degree slope. Come on. We'll get all the food and supplies we can carry from the plane, but we should hurry." I turned into the woods and quickly unfastened my backpack on the way, just in case we got caught in a slide. I wanted to be able to toss it, not have it weigh me down if I had to make a run for it.

Eleven

⚮

It took us over an hour to reach the top of the ridge. By the time we arrived, we were both exhausted and drenched in sweat. Aaron collapsed on his back and spread his arms out in the snow.

Standing over him, I took a moment to catch my breath. "You did all right," I said.

Lowering my hood to look around, I took note of the fact that we'd emerged beyond the tree line onto a rocky clearing—a good place to set up camp and light a fire to dry out our layers.

It also provided a panoramic view of the valley below where the plane had crashed. Just as I'd suspected, there was a trail of destruction through the trees. Unfortunately, much of it was now obscured by snow that fell during the blizzard the night before.

"I wonder where we are," Aaron said, sitting up. "Do we have any idea?"

I slid my pack off my shoulders and set it down on the ground. "None. But it's a clear day so we should keep our eyes and ears open for planes or helicopters. We need to be ready to signal to them when they come. The first order of business is getting this tent set up. We're in a good location here. No one could miss us."

Aaron watched me open my pack and hunt around for my water bottle.

"You seem pretty confident they're going to come," he quietly said.

"Yeah. Don't worry about it." I found my water bottle, opened the cap, took a few sips and offered it to him.

We stared at each other for a few tense seconds. I kept my thoughts to myself.

At last, he took the bottle and guzzled.

"But you see," he began to explain as he wiped his mouth, "I'm a clinical psychologist, so I'm pretty sure that what you're doing here is trying to keep me busy and distracted so I don't panic and start to freak out."

He handed the water bottle back to me.

"If I was worried about you freaking out," I replied, "I wouldn't have told you that we were standing in an avalanche death zone."

He stared at me for a long, steady moment—no doubt trying to read my expression, to get into my head.

"Just don't worry about me, okay?" he said. "I may not know how to repel down a glacier, but I have good coping skills. I'm not going to start screaming or doing anything stupid."

"I'm not worried about a thing," I assured him as I unrolled the tent and handed him a mallet. "I just want to get this tent set up.

As we set to work, I wondered if he knew I was lying.

After setting up camp, it seemed all we did for the rest of the day was sit in silence and watch the sky, listening for the distant, coveted sound of an engine propeller or helicopter blades beating against the frigid air.

There were no such sounds. It remained eerily quiet on the hilltop, hour after hour.

Surprisingly windless, it was a perfect, fresh clean winter's day. I couldn't help but wonder if I had in fact died in that plane crash and this was my version of heaven.

But no, if this was heaven, I wouldn't be sitting here with a city boy who didn't know what a crampon was. I'd be sitting with fellow climbers—*good* climbers—who had passed on before me.

Eventually, thoughts of heaven steered me back to the terrifying moments when the plane was crashing.

Please God, just give me one more chance. If you let me live, I'll do better…I won't break any more promises.

Promises to whom? Carla of course.

I couldn't help but think about what I'd walked away from years ago when I was possessed by summit fever. When all I wanted was Everest.

Then I thought about the documentary in Iceland, and how badly I wanted to be there.

"Are you married?" Aaron asked.

I leaned back against a large rock and took another sip of water. "Yeah, are you?"

"No," he replied, "but that's all I thought about when we were going down."

I'm not sure why exactly, but I was intrigued by this. I suppose I was still uncertain about what I truly wanted and what I believed was most important in life.

I didn't enjoy disappointing people. Or God—if He even existed.

Yet my personal version of heaven spoke volumes, didn't it? It certainly wasn't a house with a white picket fence.

I sat forward. "What did you think about?"

"Regrets, mostly," Aaron explained. "I wished I'd had the chance to have a family—I always wanted a son or daughter—but life didn't work out that way. Though I did come close once."

"Yeah? What happened?"

"I lived with a woman for a while when I was in grad school, but she wasn't ready for marriage. She cheated and took off. I ran into her a couple of years later. She was living with some guy with a drug problem. The last time I saw her she was a raging alcoholic. She had a kid and couldn't hold down a job. I tried to talk her into getting help but she just asked me for money to pay her rent. I probably shouldn't have, but I gave her some. Never heard from her again. I don't know where she is now."

"That sucks," I said.

Aaron nodded and squinted up at the sun.

"I stayed away from women for a long time after that," he finally said. "I always figured there was time to get my act together and then meet the right person, but you just never know when your number's going to come up."

"Tell me something I don't know," I replied, leaning back again. "It's funny, I had similar thoughts when we were going down."

Aaron waited patiently for me to elaborate. Maybe it was a learned skill—something they teach all psych majors in therapy 101—but for some reason I couldn't help myself. His quiet penetrating stare persuaded me to confess everything.

I told him all about Carla and Kaleigh and confessed my feelings of guilt for not wanting to be a husband and father.

And my guilt about always breaking my promises—even to God, who kept giving me second chances when I probably didn't deserve them.

CHAPTER

Twelve

It was the rumble that woke us—a deafening sound like rolling thunder, uninterrupted. I'm still amazed that it was Aaron who was first to get up and lower the tent zipper.

I suppose I was overly comfortable in the frozen outdoors, while he was on edge every minute of every hour and unable to sleep.

"What *is* that?" he asked as he stepped out onto the moonlit snow.

I followed him out to see what we could see. The sky was clear and the moon was full, but the ground beneath us was shaking.

"An avalanche," I told him. "Over there."

I pointed at the mist rising up from the slope.

I was thankful we were safe on higher ground.

"The plane will be completely buried," Aaron said. Then he turned and regarded me with awe. "You were right."

I nodded and returned to the tent to go back to sleep.

"I have to ask," Aaron said the next morning as he climbed sleepily from the tent. I was sitting before a fire, melting ice for water. "What does she look like?"

"Who?" I asked.

"Your wife." He sat down across from me. "You said she was the most beautiful woman you'd ever seen."

I chuckled and dug out my phone, which I'd powered up only twice since the crash—the second time to check for service up here on the ridge. Of course there hadn't been any, otherwise our situation would have been vastly different in that moment.

I'd since turned off the mobile network to avoid draining the battery.

"Want to see her?" I shaded the screen with my glove to search through my gallery.

Aaron moved around the fire to sit beside me.

Most of the pictures had been taken during various climbs around the world which, naturally, was quite impressing Aaron, but then I found the three photos from the time I spent with Carla in Boston after we were married. That was almost eight years ago.

"This is her and Kaleigh." I held the phone up for Aaron to see. "We took this picture at the Public Garden in Boston. See the swan boats in the background? We'd just gotten off a tour around the lagoon. Kaleigh loved watching the ducks paddle their little feet. She's such a cutie."

I scrolled to the picture of Carla standing on the bridge, posing like a supermodel, her long blond hair wavy and loose about her shoulders.

"Wow, you're right," Aaron said. "She is gorgeous."

I searched for the video I'd taken of her that same day when we were lying on a blanket in the shade of a giant oak. Every time I got a new phone, I uploaded the video so I'd always have it with me, but I hadn't looked at it in a while.

I clicked on the icon.

"*Hey baby...*" she said in a seductive voice. Lying on her belly, she leaned up on her elbows and looked into the camera. "*Someday I want you to buy me a house on a lake where I can plant purple flowers.*"

"*Why purple?*" I asked.

"*Because it's my favorite color. Didn't you know that?*"

I shook my head. "*What kind of house do you want?*" I asked, humoring her.

"*Something rustic.*" She spoke with a sexy, flirtatious glimmer in her eyes. "*With a screened in gazebo next to the lake so we can sleep outside on hot summer nights.*"

I reached out and tucked a lock of hair behind her ear. "*That sounds like a dream.*"

Carla inched closer to the camera lens. "*Dreams can come true, you know.*"

The video ended abruptly and I wished there was more.

"So that's her," I said to Aaron. I showed him a few pictures of my climbs and then powered down the phone and slipped it back into my jacket pocket.

He didn't comment on the climbs but bowed his head and nodded. "I see why you want to get home to her."

But did I really want that? To be honest, I'd been thinking more about the documentary that morning, wondering if our crash had been on the news. It must have been. The jet was owned by a freaking billionaire.

"Yeah," I said, not being entirely truthful. "And after all this, I think God must be trying to tell me something. It's the second time I've stared death in the eye, and it's the second time I've survived. It has to be some kind of miracle. How lucky can one man be?"

"You are definitely lucky," he replied, gesturing toward the phone in my pocket.

Was he referring to Carla, I wondered, or all the amazing climbs I'd been on?

"I guess it's time I faced up to my responsibilities," I said.

Aaron looked at me strangely. I still don't understand why.

ᴄ⳼ᴏⳆ⳼ᴏ

"What's that?" Aaron asked the next day when I emptied out my backpack onto the floor of the tent. He reached for the leather-bound book that I'd tossed aside on the sleeping bag.

"It's a journal," I told him. "I thought it would be a good idea to document what was happening in Iceland during the filming in case someone wanted to write a book about Atherton. He is a celebrity after all."

Aaron flipped through all the blank pages. "You haven't written anything yet."

"No."

He closed it and handed it back to me. "So this is going to be your contribution to a trashy tell all? How much do you hope to sell it for?"

There was no mistaking the note of disapproval in his voice.

Then I remembered he was Atherton's therapist.

"It could be an important book," I explained.

He inclined his head. "Maybe. Why don't you use it to record what's happening here? Write down your personal thoughts. Keeping a journal can be therapeutic."

"I don't need therapy," I told him.

"Of course not," he replied, "but like you said, it could be an important book. If we ever get out of here, people might want to know what happened. Or you could just keep it for yourself."

He handed me the journal and I opened it to a blank page somewhere in the middle. For a long time I thought about what he was trying to tell me.

Just keep it for myself? What would be the point of that?

We remained on the hilltop for four days, but no rescue planes came for us.

Thankfully the weather was fair with blue skies and warm sunshine, which helped to keep our spirits up, but on the fifth day we were running low on what meager food supplies we'd scavenged from the plane before the avalanche. I knew that very soon we'd have to take steps to find something.

We were also running low on matches, which I considered a more serious problem.

While we sat before the fire that night, I weighed our options.

"Tomorrow we should head down into the valley and try to catch something," I said.

Aaron lifted his gaze. "You mean like…an animal?"

"Yeah, city boy," I said with a chuckle. "I mean an animal, or maybe some fish if we can find a river."

"What about the avalanche death zone?"

I poked the fire with a stick, which sent a tiny explosion of sparks floating upward. "The worst time is twelve to forty-eight hours after a heavy snowfall, so we should be fine."

Aaron stared at the fire and said nothing for a long moment, then at last he regarded me steadily. "Shouldn't we stay here in case a rescue plane comes?"

I didn't want to say anything, but my hopes for a gallant rescue from the sky had been dwindling since day three, and I was getting hungrier by the minute. Sure, we had ice to melt for water, but we couldn't survive on just that. Heaven only knew how long it could be before we got out of there. We had to start fending for ourselves.

"The tent will be here," I said. "If there's a plane, they'll spot it. We'll leave a note about where we went."

Aaron nodded and gazed back toward the tent. "Somehow I doubt you have a fishing rod in that backpack treasure chest of yours. Or a shotgun, for that matter. I suppose you have a plan?"

I didn't—not exactly—but I wasn't about to tell Aaron that. I just hoped I'd come up with something by morning.

"Holy crap," Aaron said. "What kind of fish is that?"
"I think it's a trout," I replied, "but it's not going to be easy to catch."

We stood on the snowy bank of a wide brook, staring down at the clear water that flowed swiftly by.

"Maybe we should try for a rabbit or a squirrel," Aaron suggested. "Less chance of going for a swim."

I glanced down at my climbing boots, then took a gander at Aaron's. "You're probably right."

Turning away from the water, we ventured back into the woods.

For the greater part of the day, we wandered about in the valley, keeping an eye out for tracks in the snow that might lead us to something with protein, but the trout was the most exciting thing we encountered outside of squirrels.

"I don't think I've ever been this hungry before," Aaron said as we stopped by a grove of white birch trees with no leaves on them. "It feels like someone's clawing at the inside of my stomach."

I stopped to rest and catch my breath. "Me, too. I can't stop thinking about a juicy steak I had over Christmas. It was perfectly seared and served with a thick peppercorn sauce. Garlic mashed potatoes."

"Stop," Aaron said, holding up a hand. "You're killing me."

We started moving again.

"Let's think about this," I said as I trudged through the snow. "That trout we saw was resting in an eddy, just downstream from a narrow section in the brook. If we can fashion some sort of spear—maybe lash my knife to the end of a stick—we could probably catch one tomorrow."

"We shouldn't risk losing your knife," Aaron replied. "It's the only one we have."

I considered this and decided he was right, but there had to be a way. I stopped and looked around.

"Let's keep our eye out for a couple of saplings and cut them down, take them with us. Tonight we can strip the bark and sharpen the ends."

I scanned the woods for something suitable. Then Aaron hit me in the arm.

"Seth…look," he whispered.

I turned to see a white rabbit—actually it was probably an Arctic hare—hopping into a tangle of snowy underbrush.

"Holy shit," I whispered. "Come on!"

We both took off running.

"Here are the tracks," Aaron said, panting heavily as he pointed down at the snow. "He's heading that way."

As we moved stealthily through the trees, I slid my knife out of its sheath, ready to fling it through the air if we spotted the hare again.

We continued for more than half an hour, but lost the trail somewhere in a thicket of young spruce. By that time the sun was low in the sky.

"We're not going to catch him," I said, re-sheathing my knife. "We should head back to camp."

Only then did I realize I hadn't taken a compass reading in a while, and I didn't know which way we had come. I considered following our tracks back but that was going to be impossible in the darkness and for all I knew, we might have just run in a big circle. I looked around in all directions while Aaron watched me intently.

"Are we lost?" he asked, though he seemed to already know the answer.

"Not lost," I replied, digging out my compass. "I'm just not sure how far we traveled. Let me get a reading." I wiped the perspiration from my brow and turned my body to the left. "North is that way," I said, "so rather than follow our tracks back and risk going in a circle, we should travel in a straight line in this direction until we reach the base of the mountain."

"You're sure?" Aaron asked, regarding me with uncertainty.

"Yeah, let's go. It'll be dark soon."

I pushed past him and struggled to ignore the grumbling sensation in my stomach as I searched for a landmark to guide us.

I have no idea how far we traveled after I took that first reading, but we never did reach the base of the mountain, nor was there any visual sign of it from where we stood. I figured we must have roamed the entire length of the valley until we came out at one end.

Which end, I had no idea. It was overcast, so I couldn't even see the North Star.

"We're going to have to stop here and set up camp for the night," I said. "There's no point wandering around in the dark. We'll find our way back in the morning."

To Aaron's credit, he didn't openly question my decision or lay blame for our situation, but I knew he was frustrated. I was, too.

"The temperature's dropping fast," he said. "Let's look for shelter. There's a tree over there with low-hanging branches. What about that?"

We went to check it out. I decided it was as good a place as any because the branches touched the ground. They would form sloping walls around us.

"There's not much space under there," Aaron said.

"That's okay," I replied. "The smaller the better because it'll be easier to trap the warm air. Let's get a fire going." I turned to face Aaron. "You go and gather some fuel and I'll cut some boughs from other trees to use as bedding. But don't go too far. Make sure to keep me in sight and whistle if you get disoriented."

"I'll be fine," Aaron said as he trudged off.

I immediately got busy snapping off low-hanging limbs from nearby evergreens.

By this time, my toes were growing numb from the cold and it was getting harder to feel confident about this situation. I was starving and had no idea where we were. I didn't have a single clue—yet I was stuck playing the leader with a guy who didn't know the first thing about surviving in the outdoors.

As I hacked away at the trees with my ax, I wondered irritably if I would have been better off on my own, without having to keep an eye on Aaron. He was slowing me down and supplies were dwindling. I hated having to explain things to him—why this and not that.

Jesus. Five days. They should have come for us by now.

Aaron would freak out if he knew the doubts that were playing around in my head.

Seriously. I couldn't take much more of this.

Resolving to stay focused on my task, I returned to our tree shelter and dropped an armful of branches onto the snow. It was pitch black inside, so I opened my pack and found my flashlight. I turned it on, then I laid the boughs out as thickly as possible.

God, my feet were freezing. We needed fire. Soon. Where the hell was Aaron?

Emerging from the shelter with my flashlight, I squinted though the darkness. I shone the beam up at the treetops and noticed a light snow beginning to fall.

Great. Just what we need.

Again, I swung the beam of light around the dense forest.

"Aaron!" I called out.

I heard no reply, so I closed my eyes and listened.

Nothing seemed to be out there but the hush of the wilderness.

The sub-zero chill seeped into my bones. When I breathed, I felt a burning sensation in my lungs.

The temperature was dropping fast.

None of this felt right.

"Aaron!" I called out again. "Where are you?"

My heart began to race. It hadn't been that long since he left. He couldn't have traveled far.

Then suddenly—*a noise.* Heavy, reckless footfalls growing closer. Twigs snapping. A shadowy burst of movement caught my eye.

Thank God it was Aaron.

"What's wrong?" I asked, adrenaline flooding my veins.

He skidded to a halt. "I saw something. A pair of eyes. It might have been a wolf, but it looked more like a cat. A lynx, maybe. He was big."

I strode forward to shine a beam of light across the surrounding the area. "Where?"

He pointed. "About twenty yards away. That direction. He was just huddled in the bush, staring at me like I was something good to eat."

I saw nothing in the gloomy depths, so I turned and strode back to where Aaron stood in front of our shelter. "The fire should keep him away. Let's hurry and get it lit. I'm freezing."

"Me, too," he said, dropping the wood onto the snow.

Fifteen

I t wasn't easy to get the fire going. First we had to dig down to the bare ground, but the heat from the flames kept melting the ice that was interlaced with the frozen earth. Eventually it evaporated into the fire which sizzled, sputtered and finally went out.

We used five matches to relight it. I only had six left in my pack.

Aaron asked if I knew how to light a fire without matches, and I tried to explain how to do it. I hoped it wouldn't come to that, however.

"Maybe we'll get rescued tomorrow," I said to him, knowing full well that the odds of our being rescued now were slim at best. No one was coming for us. We were in for it now, up to our ears in shrinking chances of survival. I was seriously starting to lose it.

And I was pissed about missing the climb with George Atherton. I'd wanted to be part of that documentary.

Were they filming now? I wondered. Or were they waiting for us?

After about an hour, the wind picked up, so we had no choice but to kick snow onto the fire and retreat into the shelter.

I tried to sleep but couldn't. All my senses were highly tuned as I listened for the lynx. Or something worse.

This was nuts. I'd had enough of being stranded. I didn't want to be here. Stuck with Aaron.

And for how much longer?

All I wanted was to be somewhere else.

I t was past midnight, and there I sat with my flashlight, awake in the tree shelter, writing like crazy in my journal with no idea what would happen next. I wasn't even sure if we'd be alive in the morning.

I was still uneasy about the lynx Aaron saw. I couldn't help but imagine he was out there somewhere in the darkness, waiting to pounce.

Cats are like that. They're patient. They'll sit for hours watching their prey.

The storm worsened. Time passed slowly while the branches blew around and dumped snow on us every hour or so.

Aaron began to shiver uncontrollably and I was worried about him. I'd seen severe cases of hypothermia before and I prayed we wouldn't reach that point.

I thought about lighting a fire inside the shelter but I was concerned about ventilation and carbon monoxide poisoning and basically burning the whole tree down around us.

Although a blaze like that would make a great signal fire. I just wasn't sure there would be anyone to see it. I felt like we might as well be on the moon.

So I just kept sitting there. Listening to the wind. Listening for the lynx.

Thinking.

My hands got really cold. Numb and stiff. I could barely hold the pen. I didn't think I could write any more.

I inspected my handwriting. It was pretty bad, and I knew I should try to conserve the flashlight battery.

I decided to continue writing after we got back to camp.

God willing.

I said another prayer.

Aaron

Seventeen

After Seth and I got lost chasing the hare and spent the night under the tree in the storm, he couldn't write anymore, but he asked me to continue telling the story where he left off.

He said it helped pass the time, and I get that. Keeping a journal is a good distraction. It keeps the mind limber—so to speak.

That night, the snow continued to fall for hours, and the wind blew without mercy. It was freezing in our so-called "shelter," which dumped snow all over us every time the branches gave way to the weight. I shivered so badly I barely slept. All I could do was curl up in a tight ball to conserve my core body heat and pray for morning to come quickly.

I have no idea what time it was when those quiet hours of darkness exploded into total panic and chaos. I hadn't exactly been sleeping, but I must have been dozing because I don't remember any warning signs, no buildup to the moment when I woke to the sound of Seth screaming.

Suddenly, before I could think straight, I was wrestling with a growling, fanged creature with sharp claws—a monster that seemed to have the strength of ten men.

It all happened in a blur. The lynx must have been waiting for hours, crouched outside in the blizzard, primed to pounce, which he did with lightning speed and astonishing force. He shot through our flimsy wall of pine branches and leaped onto Seth, clawed at his face, then punctured his shoulder and arm with his teeth.

I'm not sure how long the attack lasted. It must have been only a few seconds, otherwise Seth's injuries would have been far worse.

All I remember is the blinding shock and natural instinct that drove me to grab hold of the cat and swing an ax through the air.

I must have clubbed it in the head because it screeched like the devil and flew out of the shelter.

"Aaron…are you okay?"

It was Seth asking me the question.

Strangely…as I became aware that he was speaking to me, I realized I was standing outside in the blizzard, barely conscious of the ice pellets striking my face.

I have no memory of leaving the shelter. When I looked down, I was gripping the yellow ax handle tightly in my hand. There was some blood on the tip.

It all sounds very heroic, I suppose, but in fact, I was paralyzed with fear. Terror burned through my bloodstream and rushed to my head. It's a wonder I didn't pass out.

"He's gone," Seth said, wiping a glove across his cheek. "We scared him away."

I turned to look at Seth but it was dark. I couldn't see the scratches on his face or the puncture wounds and rips on his jacket. I didn't see any of that until the next morning.

Even then, I was in another place. I barely remember noticing. At least not until much later.

—⁀ᴄ—

A strange, low hum woke me at dawn. At first I thought I was dreaming. I remember the sensation of floating. I wanted to float all the way to the sky.

Then the sound grew louder in my ears until my mind latched onto reality and I remembered where I was—lying on a bed of pine boughs under a snow-covered tree.

Lost.

Somewhere in the Canadian wilderness.

Almost certainly hypothermic.

My eyes flew open. "Seth. Do you hear that?"

I shook him awake and tried to crawl out of the shelter. As I pushed my way sluggishly through the evergreen branches, more snow fell on me and I felt the icy shock of it slide down the back of my neck. "It's a plane."

I rose heavily to my feet and looked to the sky, but the treetops obscured my view. I could only hear it…The distant, low drone of an engine and propellers somewhere above us, growing closer.

Seth emerged from the shelter. "Which way?" he asked.

"I don't know. But they'll never see us here. We have to find a clearing."

Without waiting to discuss it, I took off in a desperate, stumbling push through the forest, my movements slow and labored.

My body was unbelievably numb.

It wouldn't do what I wanted it to do.

Seth followed. He called my name, but I couldn't stop, not when a search plane had finally come for us. I had to find a way out of the woods to catch it. To signal it, somehow.

I followed the sound of the engine until I saw—not far ahead, just beyond a grove of leafless aspens—a wide-open space.

As I staggered out of a thicket onto the snow-covered field, I tore my sleeve on prickly thorns. But it didn't matter...

There it was! Just over there! Flying low to the ground!

Flying away.

Sprinting as fast as my legs would carry me, I chased the plane and frantically waved my arms over my head.

"*Stop!*" I yelled again. "*Over here!*"

The plane flew toward a mountain in the distance.

"*Come back!*" I stopped and jumped up and down, beckoning to the plane like some kind of lunatic. "*We're here!*"

Its wing dipped, then it veered sharply to the right around a high ridge and disappeared from view.

The sound of the engine grew faint. All I could do was stand there, immobile, breathing hard and staring after it, listening to the sound of the propellers until I couldn't hear them anymore. Until there was nothing left but my thunderous heartbeat in my ears, drowning out the silence of the wilderness.

Come back. Please come back. We're alive.

A squirrel chattered at the edge of the forest.

The sound of Seth's heavy footsteps across the snow caused me to turn.

"Did you see it?" he asked, stopping to bend over with his hands on his knees, panting heavily.

Only then did I notice the bloody scratch marks on his face and the slashes and tears on his jacket.

"Yes," I replied, "but we're too late. It's gone."

"Shit!" He ripped his backpack off his shoulders and threw it on the ground.

I collapsed to my knees, fell forward onto my elbows, and cradled the top of my head in the heels of my gloved hands.

Gone.

"We shouldn't have come down here," I quietly said as I rocked back and forth on my knees. "We should have stayed on the hilltop and kept a signal fire going."

"What…and starve to death?" Seth argued. Then he glared at me with derision and began to pace back and forth like a caged animal. "Don't try to pin this on me."

"I'm not pinning anything on anyone," I replied.

"Yes, you are," he said. "I can tell. All along you've done nothing but ask stupid questions and wait for me to make all the hard decisions. If I didn't feel so damn responsible for you, I would have done things differently. God knows I wouldn't be standing here right now."

My brow pulled together in a frown. "*What* would you have done differently?" I asked, rising to my feet. "It wasn't my idea to come down off the ridge. It was yours."

"We were out of food!" He jabbed a finger into my chest, pushing me backwards.

"And how is that my fault?" I asked.

Seth turned and picked up his pack. "Jesus Christ." He slung the pack over his shoulders and started walking.

"Where are you going?" I asked.

"Back to the camp," he replied, pointing toward the west. "That's gotta be it over there, just ahead. Our best hope is that the searchers saw the tent. Maybe they'll keep looking for us. We left a note, didn't we?"

I took a moment to catch my breath, then I started walking, following Seth toward the mountain pass where the plane had disappeared.

At least we'd found our way out of the woods, I told myself as I trudged through the snow. And we hadn't been eaten by a giant devil cat. Now my blood was circulating, warming my extremities. That was a good thing.

With any luck, the searchers had spotted the tent from the sky and we'd be rescued by nightfall.

Please Lord, I prayed. *Let that be what happens next.*

"I'm sure this is where it was!" Seth shouted when we reached the top of the ridge. He pointed at the ground. "The tent was right here!"

"Are you sure we're in the right place?" I asked, though I don't know why I was even asking. Everything looked exactly the same except for the fresh blanket of snow.

How then, could there be no tent? No campsite? Did this mountaintop have a doppelganger? Or did a band of thieves come and steal everything?

I gazed around with concern and managed to identify the familiar rock face and the view of the valley below. We'd spent four days up here. I was certain I knew every inch and cranny.

Seth dropped his pack and began to dig. "It was right here," he said again. "I'm positive. This is where we hammered the pegs."

I watched him dig through the snow like a terrier after a bone, fast and frantic. Then he stopped suddenly, paused, fell over and rolled onto his back. For a long time he stared up at the sky.

"No!" he sobbed. "That didn't happen."

"What?" I asked.

To my astonishment, Seth curled in a ball and wept for many minutes.

All I could do was wait quietly for him to finish.

At last he sat up and caught his breath. He spoke hoarsely. "The tent tore away from the pegs. It must have blown off in the blizzard last night." He looked to the horizon. "We shouldn't have left it."

My stomach churned with dread. Did this mean there had been no colorful signal for the rescue plane to see? Or was the tent flying somewhere else nearby, like a giant red flag, flapping at the top of a tree?

"We have to find it," Seth said, rising to his feet. "We can't survive without it. Last night was hell. I'm not doing that again."

Maybe he was referring to the lynx, or maybe just the snow falling on us, or our hopeless situation. I had no idea. I didn't get the chance to ask.

"Where are you going?" I asked as he strode across the ridge with purpose.

"I need to see if it's out there."

He began to jog, and I frowned as I watched him.

"Be careful!" I shouted. "Don't get too close to the edge!"

Thank goodness he stopped when he reached the steep side of the cliff. Carefully he leaned over to peer below, then he turned around to face me.

"I see it!" he called out. "It's just down there, caught in some trees!"

The breath sailed out of my lungs, and I bowed my head in relief.

Maybe the rescue plane spotted it after all. Maybe there's still hope.

When I lifted my gaze, Seth was leaning out again, attempting to get a better look.

I didn't enjoy heights, so I couldn't understand how he could do that, but he was a seasoned climber. He'd summited Everest five times while the most *I'd* ever done was reach the top of the

Empire State Building—by elevator. Surely he knew what he was doing.

Then something gave way. Or perhaps he just slipped. I'll never know for sure.

I stared for a long moment in disbelief. The breath sailed out of my lungs as I ran forward.

CHAPTER

Nineteen

"Seth!" I reached the edge and carefully peered over the side.

There he lay, sprawled on his back at the bottom of the ravine, about fifty feet down.

I couldn't tell if he was conscious or not, then his hand moved and he signaled to me.

"I'll be right there!"

Quickly, I dashed across the snow to fetch his backpack which contained a first aid kit and ropes and water. Knowing I couldn't reach him from the steep edge, I skidded down the gentler slope, sliding on my backside for a good part of the way.

When I reached the bottom, I ran hard and fast into the ravine.

Though I knew it had been an exceedingly bad fall, I was shocked, regardless, to find him so badly injured.

His legs were twisted grotesquely and his face was covered in blood. The scratches inflicted by the lynx the night before now seemed unimportant compared to this.

"I'm here," I said, dropping to my knees beside him.

His eyes flickered open and he turned his head to look up at me. "That was dumb," he croaked. "I shouldn't have done that."

"It's been a rough day," I gently replied, working hard to maintain my calm as I glanced down at his broken legs.

"I'm cold," he said, and began to shiver.

"Take my jacket." I quickly unzipped it, pulled it off and covered him with it. "Is that better?"

He nodded, then coughed up some blood.

Oh God...Please not this...

I have to be honest. I knew I couldn't save Seth. There was absolutely nothing I could do. He had tumbled down a steep, rocky incline, broken both his legs and probably his back, and it was obvious he was bleeding internally.

Even if I could fashion some sort of stretcher to move him, where would I take him? There was no hospital nearby. No doctors, no nurses.

Desperately, I glanced up at the sky.

God. Are you there at all? Now would be a good time to send a helicopter. Please, I'm begging you.

Nothing.

I looked back down at Seth. "What can I do?"

"Water?" he asked.

I reached into the bag, withdrew the bottle and fed him some. He tried to swallow but choked and coughed it up.

I put the water bottle away.

"Sorry about the things I said earlier," Seth muttered. "I didn't mean them."

"It's nothing," I replied. "Everything's fine now."

He nodded and lay there, blinking up at the sky. "I think I hear the plane," he said. "They must be coming for us."

I listened but heard nothing. "It shouldn't be long now," I said. Then I removed both our gloves and held his hand.

Three hours later I stood with my back against the steep rock face, staring blankly at Seth's lifeless form.

A knot had formed in the pit of my stomach. I couldn't seem to move from my spot, nor could I believe this had happened. That *any* of this had happened.

Seth was gone and I was alone now—going over and over in my head the significance of his final wishes.

What a quiet day it was. There was not a single breath of wind in the air.

I glanced up to watch a gull soar against the blue. He was white on the bottom and gray on the tops of his wings. Graceful and majestic looking.

Eventually, my mind turned to certain practicalities.

What was I to do with Seth's body? He had made his wishes clear to me, but I wasn't sure I would ever be able to carry them out.

Nevertheless, I couldn't very well leave him for the animals. Nor could I bury him because the ground was frozen solid.

In the end I decided it would be best to do as he asked: burn his remains and save his ashes. If I could, I would fulfill his wishes, or perhaps I would deliver them to his family.

After coming to that decision, my heart began to pound heavily and I felt nauseous. I slid down the wall of rock to sit on the ground, where I wept uncontrollably for a very long time.

Changes

Twenty

Sharp branches cut my cheeks as I flew through the forest, spear in hand. By this time my hunger had mushroomed into something astronomical, and I knew I could no longer continue to watch the skies and pray to be rescued. Clearly that was not to be my fate. At least not today.

Tomorrow perhaps?

Hah. Call it a gut feeling, but something told me that no one would *ever* come for me. I was here for the long haul and I had only one choice.

I could lay down and die, or I could live.

If I was going to live, I'd have to learn to take care of myself— to eat, drink and stay warm—and accept the fact that perhaps I was here alone for some reason I could not yet fathom.

Though I prayed it would be clear to me one day.

Or maybe there was no rhyme or reason to it. I was just here, like the birds and the fish. End of story.

But no. This was not to be the end of *my* story. At least not today. Not if I had any say in the matter. I was starving and weak from hunger, but I was not without intelligence and resourcefulness. I had everything Seth left to me—his compass, wallet, cellphone, a knife, two ice axes, warm clothing, water bottles and camping gear—which included the tent I had retrieved from the bush.

I'd used his knife to carve the spear which I now held in my hand.

Somehow I would find my way in and out of the forest to catch something to eat.

I would catch it, kill it, and cook it.

Which brings me back to my current predicament...

In pursuit of a white rabbit—or rather a fat Arctic hare—I was growing rather tired.

I'd spotted him on my way to the creek where I'd hoped to spear a fish. The hare caught my attention not long after I entered the woods. The instant I saw him, I threw my spear.

Naturally, I missed. I've since learned not to *throw* the spear. It only works to kill things at close range.

Anyway, he was startled by my presence and hopped into the bush, but I picked up my spear and followed.

I was fast and nimble on my feet at first, and exceedingly motivated. Though I suppose he was, too.

So I ran. Fast and hard, never losing sight of him, not for a single second. It wasn't easy, either. Those hares can move. By my estimation, he jumped as far as six feet in a single bound and traveled as fast as a car.

By some miracle I caught up to him and threw myself into the air to catch him in my arms. I had him, too. For a few brief, heart-stopping seconds I hugged him to my chest and marveled at the fact that I'd caught a rabbit. But then the slippery little rascal squirmed from my grip and I had to scramble to my feet, get on the run again.

I followed that darn rabbit out of the woods, then found myself in the presence of something quite unconceivable.

An entire herd.

There must have been a hundred of them, out in the open, under the sun, bouncing about, happily.

Imagine what a sight that was for a starving man in my position to behold.

⁓

If someone had been filming me, the footage would probably have gone viral on the Internet within a day.

I can't even picture what I must have looked like—diving through the air to catch hopping rabbits in a herd, losing one after the other. Diving again.

But I never gave up, not even when one exceptionally belligerent rabbit kicked me repeatedly in the face and gave me a bloody nose.

They can be quite vicious, I discovered.

I was so hungry, however, I felt no pain. The way they fought back only strengthened my resolve and turned me into something equally vicious—a wild man I did not even recognize.

Eventually I got a good grip on the back leg of one of them and didn't let go.

Within seconds I had snapped its neck.

The rest of the herd quickly scattered.

⁓

For reasons I don't wish to revisit, I had no matches left, but on my second night alone in the wilderness, I had taught myself how to start a fire without them. Or rather, Seth had explained it to me, the day before he passed.

It took me five hours to get that first fire going, but I stuck with it and succeeded by carving a long notch into a dry, narrow log and running a stick up and down until sparks trickled down into the tinder.

On the night of my Olympic trials with the flash mob of Arctic hares, I had dinner to cook, so there was nothing to keep me from devoting another five hours to the task of making fire.

I am pleased to report that it only took sixty minutes that night. Then it was time, at last, to roast the rabbit.

I swear, no other meal in my life ever tasted so good.

Civilization

༄

Carla

I was sitting in my car, waiting outside the ice skating rink when my cell phone vibrated in my purse. I leaned across the seat, saw that it was Gladys calling, and swiped the screen.

"Hello?"

"Carla, is that you?" she asked, sounding panicked.

"Yes, it's me."

"Where are you? I just called the apartment."

"I'm at the rink waiting for Kaleigh to finish her figure skating lesson," I replied. "She should be out soon. What's going on? Is there news?"

Long before Gladys had a chance to answer, my stomach twisted into a sickening knot, because something in me knew. I could sense this would not be the call I'd been hoping for.

"They've called off the search," Gladys said with a sob. "How could they do that? It's only been a week. What if he's still alive out there?"

I closed my eyes and bowed my head. "I'm so sorry, Gladys."

Balling my hand into a fist, I pounded it against the upholstered armrest of the car door—though I can't say I was surprised by Gladys' news.

For a week they had been searching off the northern coast of Newfoundland—which was where the pilots had last radioed a distress call—but there had been no sign of wreckage anywhere. With each passing day, I'd lost a little more hope because all evidence pointed to the fact that the aircraft had run into trouble somewhere over the ocean. The plane was most likely sitting at the bottom of the ice-cold sea. Case closed.

I was startled when someone knocked on the passenger side window of my car. It was Kaleigh, trying to open the locked door.

Quickly I pushed the button to unlock it and wiped the tears from my cheeks.

"Gladys? Kaleigh just got in the car. I'll have to call you back. I'm sorry. I'm sorry about everything."

I ended the call.

"What's going on?" Kaleigh asked.

I told her the news.

This time she cried, and I admit, I was relieved to see her shed some tears.

Then she confessed something to me. "I didn't want to tell you this," she said, "but I already knew he was gone."

"What? *How?*"

Her tear-glistened eyes met mine. "I dreamed about it."

Turning in my seat, I looked at her directly. "What did you dream?"

"That he came to say good-bye, and he said he was sorry for not being a good dad. It wasn't scary or anything. That's why I didn't wake you."

I laid my hand on her knee. "I can't believe you didn't tell me this."

"I thought it was just a dream," she replied. "Maybe it was, but I was pretty sure he was going to heaven."

That night, I met Audrey for dinner at a popular wild game restaurant downtown. Kaleigh had been invited for a sleepover at her Aunt Nadia's house.

Audrey was my half-sister-in-law because she'd been married to my half-brother Alex, who I'd only met a few weeks before he was killed on the job as a firefighter.

Audrey and I became close after meeting for the first time—which was almost ten years ago. Her daughter Wendy was like a sister to Kaleigh, and the two of them were sleeping over at her Aunt Nadia's place, with Nadia's daughter Ellen.

We often referred to Ellen, Wendy, and Kaleigh as our Three Musketeers.

"How are you holding up?" Audrey asked when the waitress brought our menus.

"It's been tough," I replied, keeping my gaze lowered. "I still can't believe he's really gone, and yet at the same time I can. Kaleigh had a dream about it. But even so, there's something in me…It's hard to describe. I just feel like he's still out there. That it's not over."

I picked up the menu and looked it over, not entirely paying attention to the descriptions. I just needed time to pause, because it was difficult to talk about Seth. The wounds were still so raw.

After I chose something to order, I set the menu aside.

"It's going to be hard to let go," Audrey said. "You were together—well, *sort* of together—for a long time."

"I hate not knowing what really happened," I said. "It haunts me sometimes when my imagination takes over."

Audrey set her menu down as well. "Maybe you should talk to someone about it, like a grief counselor. They can be really helpful. And how about Kaleigh? How's she dealing with all this?"

I sat back in my chair and stared off toward the bar at the back of the restaurant. "She's doing surprisingly well," I replied, "but that's not necessarily a good thing. I just wish she had gotten to know Seth better. I always thought, maybe someday, he would get tired of climbing and come home to Boston and settle down. Even if we weren't together as man and wife, I sometimes dreamed that he'd be around to develop a closer relationship with her. But now that will never happen. She'll never know what it feels like to have a real dad."

"You don't know what the future holds," Audrey reminded me optimistically. "You were always very loyal to Seth, but now that he's gone, maybe you'll meet someone." She quickly covered her mouth with a hand. "Oh God, that was so insensitive. I'm sorry, I have foot-in-mouth disease."

I rested my elbows on the table. "Don't worry about it. It's not like I've never thought about having a relationship again. Seth and I may have still been legally married, but practically speaking, we'd been separated for a long time." I glanced down at Audrey's wedding ring and felt uneasy about asking the question, but I had to know. "How long was it, after Alex died, before you felt ready to be with someone else?"

She took a deep breath and let it out. "Alex was gone for two years when I fell for David."

I quickly shook my head to clear any thoughts of moving on. It was too soon anyway. There were still so many emotions to deal with.

The waitress came to take our orders, and after she was gone, I leaned back in my chair. "It's going to take me awhile to get over this. I can't imagine a life where Seth doesn't exist. I know we had our problems, but I did love him."

"I know you did," Audrey replied, "even when some of us wanted to shake you."

I raised my water glass to my lips. "I always admired your honesty, even when it was tough to hear." I set my water glass down again. "Did you know he had a cabin up in Maine? It was close to one of the ski hills."

"Did he own it?" she asked.

I gave her a look. "Seth...owning property? No. He was renting it, and I hope I don't have to buy out the lease. Seriously, I don't even know what's up there. All his belongings I suppose. We're going to have to clear it all out when we work through his estate. That's going to be hard."

Audrey leaned forward and spoke carefully. "I'm sorry, Carla, but I have to ask. Did he have life insurance?"

I recognized the concern in her eyes, because she knew the situation. The only reason I was able to work part-time at the bank was because Seth sent me money a few times a year, and it was usually a decent sum.

It had always been important to me that I be at home for Kaleigh as much as possible. When she was younger, I didn't want to put her in full-time daycare. Sure, I needed help sometimes—my neighbor across the hall had always been particularly kind. She was the grandmotherly type who baked cookies and took Kaleigh to the museum.

"Yes, thank goodness," I replied, reaching for my water again. "We talked about that when I got pregnant and we each got life insurance policies. The amount of his fund should keep me going until she's at least eighteen."

The waitress brought our salads.

"That's a relief," Audrey said, picking up her fork. "But please, if you ever need help, just let us know. Garry and Jean will be there for you as well. You know that, right?"

I nodded, because Jean was Alex's mom, and she considered herself Kaleigh's great aunt, even though they weren't actually related by blood, as I was only Alex's half-sister. But that didn't matter. They were like family to Kaleigh and me. We were blessed to have them in our lives.

I sighed. "We still have the memorial service to plan. Gladys won't be much help. She's taking it pretty hard. He was her only child."

Audrey shook her head. "No parents should ever have to outlive their child."

"So true."

We continued to chat about plans for the memorial service—what music we would select, what photographs we'd display. Then Audrey talked about her work for a little while.

I was grateful for the change of subject. Sometimes it helped to talk of other things.

Soon, our main courses arrived and when the waitress set my plate down in front of me, I closed my eyes and breathed in the delectable scent of the moist, juicy, slow-roasted meat.

I took my time picking up my fork, inspecting the presentation.

After one bite, I felt some of the tension drain out of my shoulders, then I leaned back to appreciate the flavors. "Wow. This is amazing. Seriously. I've never tasted anything so good in my life."

"What in the world did you order?" Audrey asked with a penetrating stare.

I closed my eyes and swallowed. "It's the roasted rabbit."

⸎

"I don't understand," I said to the man on the phone as I paced around my kitchen. "We've had those policies for years. Seth told me exactly how much his was worth."

"When was the last time you spoke to him about it?" the man asked.

I had to stop and think. Seth and I had rarely communicated over the past couple of years. "I'm not sure. I can't remember."

The man paused. "I'm sorry, Ms. Matthews. I wish I had better news for you."

I felt my blood begin to boil. No, this couldn't be right...

"You're telling me he cashed out the entire thing? How is that possible? I never knew that was an option."

"Well, it's not an option for *you*," he said, "because you purchased what's called a term life policy. That means if you cancel it and stop paying the premiums, you are no longer covered from that moment on. What Seth purchased was a whole life policy, which is more like an investment with a cash value that you can withdraw at any time. He cancelled the policy before Christmas and received a check from us."

I sank down onto the chair in my kitchen. "He told me he got a corporate sponsor for his trip to Everest this year. He said they were paying him twenty-five thousand dollars."

"That's about the amount of the check we mailed out," the man explained.

I felt slightly ill as I remembered the extravagant gifts Seth had bought us for Christmas. He got Kaleigh an iPhone (which I was against because I felt she was too young) and bought me a pair of diamond earrings.

'You shouldn't have,' I'd said, having no idea that he had been lying to me about where the money came from.

I couldn't help but wonder what else he had lied to me about during our marriage.

"I can't believe this." I felt betrayed. Foolish.

"Again, I'm sorry Ms. Matthews," the man on the phone said. "I wish there was something I could do."

"It's not your fault. Thank you." With that, I hung up.

For a long time I stared at the wall and thought about what I made each week working part-time at the bank. It wasn't much, but with the little extra that Seth had been sending, I was at least able to be at home with Kaleigh after school and on evenings and weekends.

Now, without Seth's life insurance policy to fall back on, how would we ever get by?

Wilderness

After a week on the ridge, I decided it was time to travel. There was no sense just sitting there, venturing down to the valley each day to catch food. That couldn't be the sole purpose of my existence—to feed myself until I grew hungry again.

And I certainly had no desire to stay there forever and die alone. I wanted to go home. So, no matter how long it took—even if I had to walk a thousand miles—I would do it. Time had a habit of marching on regardless. I might as well get somewhere.

Hence, when I woke to a clear blue sky the next morning, I packed up all my belongings and hiked down the mountain.

Which way to go? I wondered as I descended into the valley below. *East? West? North? South?*

Since I believed, based on the time of the crash, that I was somewhere in Newfoundland, I determined that a straight line to the south would be the best option.

Sliding Seth's compass out of its leather case, I took a careful look around, then established a field bearing and picked out a series of landmarks along my chosen route.

Just before I slid the compass back into the case, however, I paused. Something in my heart moved me to flip it over. I don't know what it was. I still can't explain the feeling, except that I knew with astonishing conviction that there was a message there. It practically called out to me.

So you'll always find your way home. Love Carla

Yes, I thought with a buoyancy that caught me off guard and sent a flock of butterflies fluttering into my belly.

Yes. This compass will guide me home.

I will make it.

Sliding the precious instrument back into the case, I began to walk south.

Two days later, I found myself standing on a barren, windswept coastline somewhere on the edge of the North Atlantic. Below me lay a choppy gray sea dotted with slabs of broken ice slowly floating by. It was a haunting landscape of snow-covered granite and sandstone, and the fierce wind nearly knocked me over as I stared hopelessly out at an ocean that seemed to go on forever.

Where in the world was I?

Could this be the Strait of Belle Isle, between Labrador and Newfoundland? Or was this the eastern tip of the Great Northern Peninsula? Or somewhere else?

Perhaps, if I followed this coastline, I might eventually reach a fishing village.

The possibility of that filled me with a sense of purpose and direction. It was a concrete, achievable goal, and I was pleased to have one, for I believed in my heart that I was not yet done with this life. There was still something more for me. Something important.

Though I couldn't yet define it, I could feel it, and whatever it was, I needed to get home to it.

Carefully, I leaned out over the edge of the cliff to see what lay below. A narrow rocky beach was home to a few pudgy walruses, sunning themselves on flat, wet slabs of rock.

Maybe I could gather some seaweed, I thought, which would provide me with vitamins and minerals for my journey. The way down didn't look too arduous, for further along the ridge there was a gentle, rocky slope that led to the beach.

I sat down for a moment to rest, turned by back to the biting wind, drank some water, then stood up again and headed down.

Hindsight is always twenty-twenty, of course, but I wish now that I had remained on the top of the cliff.

A short while later, I was crouching over a shallow pool of crystal-clear seawater in between the rocks, gathering kelp, when all the hairs on the back of my neck stood on end. I don't know what alerted me to the danger. Maybe it was something primeval inside me.

Instinct told me to remain still and listen. I heard the gentle lapping of the waves against the rocks. A seagull called out to me from high in the sky. Then I heard a terrible squeal further down the beach where the walruses were lounging about, and I knew there was trouble.

Swiveling on one knee, I turned to see a polar bear—he must have been at least seven feet long, close to a thousand pounds—attempt to tackle an equally large walrus that was shuffling in a panic toward the water's edge.

Unable to sink his jaws into the thick blubber, the bear backed off and paced impatiently along the shoreline, searching for a smaller, more realistic meal.

More than a little aware that *I* was a smaller, more realistic meal, I slowly crawled away from the water's edge so as not to attract the bear's attention, picked up my backpack, and hurried in the opposite direction.

As soon as I was a safe distance away, I turned to see the bear dragging a smaller walrus, most certainly dead by now, out of the water and up the beach to feast on.

Overtaken by fear and panic, I began to run. I knew that I was heading in the wrong direction, toward the north, but I'd sort that out later. All that mattered, in those blinding seconds of self-preservation, was escaping the gruesome and bloody devouring that was going on behind me.

I scrambled over some large wet rocks, rounded a bend and found myself in a small cove where the beach ended abruptly with a vertical wall of rock. There was no way around it unless I had a boat—which I didn't—and as bad luck would have it, the tide was coming in.

I glanced up at the steep stony cliffs and realized the only way to avoid being swept out to sea with the oncoming tide was to turn around and go back. Find another way off the beach.

I wondered if the bear had eaten his fill by that point. Maybe he'd be gone. I prayed it would be so.

Rounding the bend slowly, I peered out from behind the rock face to check on the herd of walruses.

Everything appeared calm. They were back, sunning themselves again, and I saw no sign of the huge bear.

Nevertheless, my heart pounded wildly as I maneuvered around some fat boulders and stepped over the slippery terrain.

Soon I was able to walk at a brisk pace toward the gently sloping path where I had descended from the ridge originally.

I noticed a thick pool of blood on the rocks where the bear had gobbled up the young walrus.

With a blast of adrenalin pumping through my veins, I picked up my pace and hurried along the beach. Soon the path was within sight, but I kept my eyes and ears attuned for anything.

I was nearly there when a strange sound from somewhere behind me caused me to stop. It resembled a cow moaning in pain, and my heart sank.

Turning slowly, I found myself trapped in the bear's ferocious gaze.

He stood on the beach about twenty yards away. The white fur around his mouth and front paws was stained with blood.

Suddenly he roared at me.

Maybe it was the wrong thing to do, but I was so terrified, I bolted. I ran faster than I'd ever run in my life, though I'd never been pursued by a polar bear before.

It was yet another first. One of many to come.

⁓

Scrambling up the path, I didn't stop to look back until I reached the top of the ridge. Then I turned.

He was still chasing me!

Briefly, I considered dropping my pack so I could run faster, but I couldn't possibly survive without it and the thought of coming back for it didn't appeal to me either. So I sprinted like a son of a bitch across the snow covered rocks while the bear growled with exasperation, halfway up the path.

I don't know what suicidal notion came over me, but I headed straight for the opposite edge of the ridge and took a flying leap over the side. One would think I'd had a parachute strapped to my back.

The next thing I knew, I was sliding down the stony slope on my backside, screaming my head off, tumbling head over heels like a bouncing ball, smacking into a few jagged boulders along the way.

I must have hit my head at some point because I have no memory of reaching the bottom. All I remember is regaining consciousness.

Slowly I sat up and looked around. I was surrounded by low-lying, snow-covered evergreen shrubs shivering in the wind.

The bear?

Apparently he had elected not to pursue me down the slope, which came as a great relief, of course.

Until the excruciating pain began.

When it didn't let up, I wondered if I might have been better off if he'd followed.

As I limped across the snowy ground toward a patch of stunted spruce trees that would offer some cover from the wind, I wondered if my positive thinking and cheerful optimism had been simply a big crock of stupid naiveté.

I felt totally defeated by Mother Nature. Even my spirit felt bruised. As for physical damage, my tooth had gone through my lip and I was spitting out blood. On top of that, my entire head was throbbing. I suspected I'd cracked a cheekbone and might have even fractured my skull.

All I wanted to do was lie down and not move a muscle until the spring thaw.

Before long, I came to a large spruce that must have toppled in a storm, or been struck by lightning. It was resting against another tree which provided a sheltered area beneath.

Dropping to my knees, I crawled under the splayed branches and hid next to the massive trunk.

I knew I couldn't lie on the snow all night or I'd freeze to death, so I pulled a few items out of the pack—the rolled up tent and the sleep pad—and lay down on top of everything.

I made no fire that night. All I could do was lie still and try to heal—and pray that the bear was not watching me from the darkness like the lynx.

As luck would have it, it began to snow.

At the time I thought I was cursed, but later I came to realize it was a blessing in disguise, because that fresh blanket of snow buried the trail of blood I'd left behind.

Twenty-six

The night I spent under the tree after running from the bear was one of my worst nights in the wilderness. It came only second to the night after Seth fell into the ravine.

Though perhaps one could argue that my polar bear night—accompanied by a cracked jaw and bloody lip—was a crucial turning point in my life because that's when the seeds of my future were planted.

It probably sounds crazy, and in my line of work, if I were hearing this story now, I would try and educate the patient by suggesting that sometimes a person can retreat into fantasy in order to seek comfort or escape an unpleasant reality.

No question, that's exactly what I did that night.

In my case, however, I have no regrets about my so-called escape from reality, because I'm not sure I would have survived the next year without more of the same.

It was exceedingly dark and cold that night, no moon or starlight at all, and I was in so much pain I couldn't sleep.

Loneliness hit fast and hard. All I wanted was to be back in my warm bed at home, even if I was tossing and turning, or at the coffee shop once again chatting with the clerks in the morning. I imagined our conversation and the feel of the hot paper cup in my hand as I slipped it into the cardboard sleeve.

A hot beverage is one of those simple things in life we don't appreciate nearly enough. I swore that, if I was ever lucky enough to set another kettle onto a stove to boil, I would never take it for granted again.

It was dark in the woods. There is no other darkness like it anywhere, and I feared I might simply expire from loneliness.

In an effort to ward off such wretched thoughts, I did something proactive instead. I dug into the pack to search for Seth's phone.

There was barely any battery life left, but enough at least for me to scroll through his photo gallery and search for the pictures of his wife in the park on that hot summer day in Boston with the swan boats in the background. That woman had inscribed his compass with words I could not let myself forget: *So you'll always find your way home.*

I needed to hear her voice.

At last I found the video Seth had shown me, and I pressed play.

There she was. *Carla,* with that cute, flirty smile.

Her eyes were impossibly blue. I exhaled with a feeling of calm, and it helped to stop the shivering.

"Someday I want you to buy me a house on a lake where I can plant purple flowers..."

I watched that video over and over until the battery died. Then I rummaged through Seth's wallet and found the printed photograph of Carla. Because my own wallet and phone had been lost in the crash, it was the only picture I had of another human being. I stared at it for a long while, then slipped it back into the wallet and put it in my pocket.

That night, I fell asleep dreaming of the house on the lake with purple flowers.

Looking back on it, I now believe that God had not forsaken me after all. On that particular night, he was definitely paying attention.

Loneliness

Carla

I never did tell Gladys about how Seth cashed in his life insurance policy and left us with nothing but his personal belongings, because I couldn't bear to tarnish her memory of Seth as a brave mountain climber and devoted father. Nor did I want her to know how Kaleigh and I had been struggling over the past few years—because there was nothing she could do about it anyway. She wasn't any better off than we were.

On one particular night as I lay in bed tossing and turning, feeling guilty about my anger towards Seth on so many different occasions, I came to a decision that I would ask my boss if I could be considered for full-time work at the bank. Maybe I could even work my way up to a clerk's position. I already knew the bank's daily operations inside out, and I certainly needed the money.

I felt good about that decision because I believed it was important to take the initiative in difficult situations and not simply drift along in the current. To have a goal would help.

Nevertheless, I was still unable to sleep. Though I'd cranked the heat up full blast, there was an inescapable chill in the air that night, so I slid out of bed, donned my slippers and fuzzy robe, and went to the kitchen to make a cup of hot chamomile tea.

While I waited in the silence for the kettle to boil on the stove, I stared at the kitchen wall and tried to recall happier times with Seth. I thought about the day we walked to the Public Garden and went for a ride on the swan boats. That was probably our best day. I was so in love with him back then, bursting with hope and optimism. I truly believed he would stay and we would become a real family. Oh, how I'd wanted it to be so.

The kettle boiled and I turned around to pour the steaming hot water into my oversized mug, then took hold of the string and dipped the tea bag up and down.

What a pleasure it was to make tea on a cold night like this.

When it was fully steeped, I moved into the living room and sat on the sofa to watch some late night television.

Mindlessly, I flicked through the channels, then settled on *The Tonight Show.*

As I cupped the warm mug in my hands and blew on it to cool it, a strange feeling came over me.

Sometimes I swore I could feel him out there in the cold, and I felt the chill inside myself. It was a strange feeling because in my heart I knew Seth was gone, but sometimes I still felt *something*— as if he were calling to me, or as if *I* was the one who was lost out there, lonely and shivering in the frigid, unforgiving North.

Why was I feeling this way? Was it possible Seth *wasn't* dead? What if he was still out there somewhere, surviving and praying to be rescued? What if he was hurt?

Suddenly I was overcome by a terrible sense of loneliness and didn't know how to fix it. The tension made my jaw ache and I laid a hand on my cheek, stroking the pain gently away.

The Tonight Show continued, but I was barely able to focus on the opening monologue. I kept thinking of that one perfect day in the park when everything was so lush and green. When I felt it was possible that my husband would stay. I replayed those memories over and over in my mind.

A house on a lake, with purple flowers...

Moving On

Carla

Six months after we held the memorial service for Seth, Jane—one of the temps at the bank where I now worked full-time—expressed her condolences over my loss, then immediately asked if she could fix me up with her older brother, who was widowed as well.

"I'm sorry," I said. "I'm not ready for anything like that."

Though it was true that Seth hadn't been gone that long, I had essentially been separated from him for quite some time before his plane went down, and for years had considered myself single. So, why I didn't feel ready to date, I'm not sure.

I'd always imagined I would love again someday, ever since it became likely that Seth was not coming home to us and I would eventually divorce.

I also imagined that the person who would come into my life would be decent and reliable, a family man who would appreciate the love he had at home and not take it for granted. For once I wanted to be someone's whole world, and I wanted that someone's passion to be for Kaleigh and me, not some mountain on the other side of the world. Was that too much to ask?

Those were fantasies, I knew, but how could I ever expect any of it to come true if I kept refusing even to go out on a date? Who was I being faithful to? No one. There was no one in my life now. It was time to stop acting like I was in a relationship.

"I apologize," Jane said awkwardly as she sat down on the stool at her teller station next to mine. "I shouldn't have suggested it."

"No worries," I assured her. "I think I just need to get my head around the idea of starting over. Tell me about your brother."

Since it was quiet in the bank and there were no customers, Jane was able to tell me that he was forty-seven years old, incredibly fit and good looking. "Imagine Matt Damon," she said. "But not like Jason Bourne. He's like the guy in the zoo movie."

That sounded promising.

"He has two grown children," Jane continued, "who are both in grad school, and he works for the IRS. But don't let his job scare you. He's lots of fun and has a great sense of humor. He loves movies and enjoys eating out. Makes his own wine."

"He sounds like a great guy," I said. "I'm surprised he hasn't been snapped up."

She rolled her eyes. "Unfortunately, women throw themselves at him all the time. I don't know what it is about handsome widowers. He's like catnip for every woman he talks to. They all want to bring him casseroles and clean his house. I can't stand it and neither can he. He doesn't like rejecting people."

I laughed. "It doesn't sound like that bad of a situation."

Jane shrugged. "No, I guess not, but I'd just like to see him end up with a woman who doesn't have an agenda." Then she pointed a finger at me. "I love the fact that you said you weren't ready. You're just what he needs, because he says the same thing to me all the time."

A customer came in and I took his deposit.

"Maybe the best thing would be to talk to us both again when we *are* ready," I said to Jane after the customer left the bank.

"When will that be?" she asked.

I thought about it for a moment, then let out a sigh. "I don't know. I must need therapy."

Jane reached over and squeezed my hand.

That night when I dropped Kaleigh off at the rink, the coach saw me in my car and waved me over. She asked me to come inside for a chat in the office.

My stomach lurched as I pulled into a parking spot and turned off the engine. Closing my eyes, I let my forehead rest on the steering wheel, then gathered my courage and got out.

A few minutes later I knocked on her open door.

"Hi Carla," she coolly said. "Come in and have a seat."

I moved to the chair in front of the desk, but she remained standing.

"I hope it's okay for me to say this," she said, leaning back against the window sill and folding her arms across her chest, "but I'm aware that you've had a rough time these past few months."

Of course she would know. Seth's disappearance had been all over the news. There had even been a Facebook page set up as a fundraiser to help Kaleigh and me, but the donations stopped coming in after about a week when a new political scandal broke and everyone forgot about the small private plane that had crashed somewhere up north.

There was some talk about a lawsuit, because George Atherton certainly had the funds to offer settlements. I'd spoken to a lawyer, but everything moved so slowly.

"It hasn't exactly been a cake walk," I replied.

She nodded, then reached for a piece of paper on the desk and handed it to me. "Your last pre-authorized payment bounced. This is the third time it's happened since January. I'm not sure what to say."

I stared at the notice and swallowed uneasily. "We've been a bit strapped."

"I get that," she said, "and I really want to help. That's why I haven't mentioned it before now. I was hoping you'd get things straightened out."

"I'm trying," I replied. "I'm working full time now."

"That's good to hear." She paused. "Is there any way you can make sure the next payment goes through?"

"There are a few calls I can make," I replied as I leaned forward and placed the sheet of paper back on her desk.

"You can keep that," she said.

With a half-smile and a nod, I rose from the chair and slid the notice into my purse. "Thanks for cutting me some slack," I said. "It's been tough, to say the least, but this skating club has been so good for Kaleigh—keeping her busy. I don't want to lose this."

She gave me a look of compassion, or maybe it was pity. "Just try to make sure the next payment doesn't bounce, okay?"

I nodded and walked out, then sat in the car for the rest of the hour, contemplating my options while I waited for Kaleigh to finish her practice. Maybe I could get rid of our home phone and just keep our cell phones. And I should make more of an effort to clip coupons to use at the grocery store.

I really didn't want to ask Garry and Jean for more money. They'd been very generous, helping me pay for the lawyer, but I did have my pride.

At the end of the hour, Kaleigh got into the car and threw her skates on the floor. "I hate my coach!" she said.

"Why? What happened?" I asked with a frown.

"She said I wasn't trying hard enough. That I was slacking off and I didn't appreciate what I had."

"Why would she say that?" I asked, wanting to march right back in there and ask the coach myself.

Kaleigh let out a huff and rested her forehead in a hand. "It doesn't matter."

"Yes, it does. Tell me what happened. Do I need to go talk to her?"

Heaven help me, if the coach was punishing Kaleigh for my bounced checks, I would have a few words to say to her about that.

"No!" Kaleigh replied. "I just want to go home. Let's get out of here. I'm sick of this place."

She'd always loved skating. Hearing her complain so bitterly was disappointing, to say the least.

"Do you want to talk about it?" I asked.

"No," she replied, "I just want to go home." Kaleigh immediately whipped out her phone and began texting.

Deciding that I would call the coach later tonight and get to the bottom of the problem, I shifted into reverse and drove out of the parking lot.

Ten minutes later, only a few blocks from home, we were crossing an intersection on a green light when a huge tractor trailer came speeding through.

It all happened so fast, I didn't even have time to hit the brakes.

The driver blared his horn. His tires screeched across the pavement. All I remember seeing was his shiny front grill to my left as he smashed into the rear passenger door behind me and sent us spinning.

⌐✑⌐

Kaleigh and I had both been wearing our seatbelts, so we remained strapped in as the car spun 360 degrees and slid across the intersection. My front end took out the back bumper on another car that had the misfortune to be in our path, but other than that, miraculously, there were no other vehicles involved.

As soon as we came to a jarring halt next to a light post, I turned to Kaleigh. "Oh, my God! Are you okay?"

She was braced rigidly against the seat, her eyes wide open in terror, gripping the door with one hand. She nodded quickly.

"Are you sure?" I asked, and she nodded again.

My heart was thrashing against my ribcage like a wild animal.

Someone knocked on my window and I jumped.

"Are you okay in there?" the man asked.

With trembling hands, I pressed the button to lower the window, which still worked, surprisingly. "I think so."

A woman ran up to the other window. "Anyone hurt? I'm a nurse."

"I think we're okay," I replied. "Kaleigh are you sure you're okay?"

"I'm fine," she replied.

I turned my eyes back to the nurse. "We're just shaken up."

"No wonder," she said. "He slammed you pretty hard. You should still be checked out. You should go to the hospital."

"Is the other driver okay?" I asked.

She glanced back at the eighteen wheeler, which had jack-knifed in the center of the intersection after he hit us.

"He just hopped out of the cab," she said. "He looks fine."

I breathed a sigh of relief. "Good."

Suddenly I heard the wail of sirens, and two cop cars skidded to a stop nearby.

"What do you mean it was my fault?" I asked the officer after I finished describing what had occurred. "The truck went through the red light. Not me."

The officer's gaze lifted and he studied my expression.

I studied his in return. He looked to be in his mid-thirties and seemed a bit macho. I suspected he worked out in the gym a lot. Maybe he was into body building.

"The driver of the other vehicle said it was the other way around," he said. "That *you* were the one who went through the red light. You haven't been drinking, have you?"

I stared at him in shock. "Of course not. He came out of nowhere and rammed into my back end."

Kaleigh approached after being checked out by the nurse and took hold of my hand.

"Did *you* see what happened?" I asked her. "The truck went through a red light. Didn't he?"

She looked up at me uncertainly. "I…I'm not sure."

I felt my forehead crinkle with concern, because all of a sudden, I wasn't sure either. I had definitely been distracted during the drive home.

Glancing to my left, I saw the man who had been first to knock on my car window. He was describing what happened to a different police officer, and another cop was taking photographs of the scene.

"What are the other witnesses saying?" I asked. Then I leaned in to read the cop's badge. "Officer..."

"Wallace," he finished for me. "So far they all say it was you who went through the red light."

I met his concerned gaze and felt something inside me crumble. Then I looked down at my shoes, shut my eyes and shook my head. "I guess I'm not sure. Maybe it *was* me."

Kaleigh squeezed my hand. "Was it our fault?" she asked.

"Not *your* fault," I replied. "*My* fault. I wasn't paying close enough attention."

"Were you talking on a cell phone or texting?" Officer Wallace asked.

"No, nothing like that. It's just been a rough year, that's all."

He wrote down what I said.

Feeling completely defeated, I leaned back against the side of my car—the front part that wasn't smashed in—and wished I could press the rewind button on that day.

"Are you feeling all right?" the cop asked. "Maybe you should sit down."

"I'm okay," I replied, though I did feel a bit lightheaded. "I'm just upset with myself. People could have been killed."

"Well..." He lowered the clipboard to his side. "It was an accident, and accidents happen to the best of us. Just be thankful that everyone's fine, and remember that your car can be replaced. You can't. The way I see it, your star was shining today."

Somehow I managed a half-smile. "You're a glass half-full kind of guy?"

"Yes, because when everybody walks away from a wreck, it's a good day." His attention turned to the tow truck that was now backing up behind my car. The engine roared noisily.

Officer Wallace took hold of my elbow to lead me out of the way. "Step over here, please."

"This is probably totaled, isn't it?" I said as I inspected the damage to my car. The whole back end was creamed and the tires were completely mangled.

"Most likely," Officer Wallace replied. "You definitely won't be driving this anywhere today. I hope you have good insurance. Why don't you grab what you need out of your vehicle and I'll take you and your daughter to the hospital. You should both get checked out."

He held up a hand to tell the tow truck operator to give us a moment.

"Kaleigh, go grab your skates." I returned to the car, opened the door and reached inside for my purse and sunglasses, while Kaleigh hurried around to the other side. I had to lean across the driver's seat to rifle through the glove compartment for the papers I would need. I decided to leave the empty coffee cup in the drink holder.

When we had everything we needed and had cleared out of the way, Kaleigh and I paused to watch the tow truck driver loop a chain around the axle. Then we followed Officer Wallace to his paddy wagon.

"Say good-bye to that car," I said to Kaleigh, "because we'll be driving it again. And let me just say that I'm very proud of you."

"What for?" she asked.

"For keeping your cool. You were incredibly brave."

"Was I?" she replied. "That's a surprise, because I was never so scared in my life."

Not long after we left the accident scene, Officer Wallace asked me why I'd been having a rough year.

I glanced over my shoulder to check on Kaleigh in the back seat. She was texting her friends, or probably Tweeting that she was riding in a cop car.

I told him about Seth dying in a plane crash.

His eyebrows lifted. "Wait a second. You were married to the mountain climber? That was *you*?"

I nodded.

"When was that?" he asked. "Like eight months ago? God, that *is* rough. I'm sorry. Did they ever find the wreckage?"

"No," I replied. "They called off the search after about a week. It was really difficult."

"It must have been," he said. "Were you able to have any kind of memorial service?"

My mind flashed back to the day when we all gathered at the church to say good-bye. There had been no coffin. All we had was a giant black-and-white photograph of Seth displayed on a shiny brass easel. He'd been climbing a glacier somewhere in New Zealand and had removed his goggles to smile for the camera.

"Yes," I replied. "We held a nice service about four months ago. It was supposed to give us closure, but I still can't stop thinking about the crash. I'm desperate for answers about where it happened and why. It's terrible that we never found out. And where no bodies were recovered…" I stopped myself. "God, I'm sorry, Officer Wallace. I shouldn't be talking like this. How depressing."

"Don't apologize," he said. "And call me Josh."

Thankful for his understanding, I sighed and looked out the window at the houses passing by and wondered why I sometimes believed that Seth and I weren't done yet. That this wasn't over.

Strangely, that feeling had begun to intensify in the past month or so. Every time I felt it, I wondered if something unexpected was about to happen. I was always waiting for the phone to ring.

I didn't know it at the time, but the phone *would* ring just a couple of weeks later.

Laughter

Carla

A few weeks after my car accident, I picked up the new replacement vehicle I'd ordered from the dealership and congratulated myself for having good insurance—though my premiums did go up.

Kaleigh loved the new car but was growing increasingly disinterested in figure skating. She begged me to let her quit and take guitar lessons instead.

After some discussion about the importance of personal growth and seeing something through, even when it was difficult, she won me over by making an excellent case for the importance of following your dreams. In the end, and partly because guitar lessons were so much more affordable than figure skating, I agreed to let her quit.

The very next day, I enrolled her in a weekly group guitar lesson with the promise of private lessons after Christmas if she enjoyed it and practiced every day. I also went online and found what I thought to be a decent instrument—second hand of course.

Kaleigh came with me to pick it up and began teaching herself some basic chords that same night.

᷍ᴄ

As it turned out, Kaleigh loved playing that guitar and I was delighted by the fact that it was more interesting to her than her cell phone. She used the home computer to print off simple sheet music and learned songs that were popular on the radio, and she practiced every night until her fingers were bruised and callused. They soon toughened up, however, and by the second month, she was playing some impressive rock classics.

Before long, she was constantly begging for private lessons, and I was keen to support her because I was pleased to see her so engaged in something. Not only did it fuel her creativity, it kept her off Twitter, where a daily landslide of middle school drama prevailed.

I promised her that if she stuck with her group lessons until Christmas, I would enroll her in a private class in January.

"But it's only October," she complained at the supper table. "I'm way ahead of everyone else in the group. It's so boring when I have to wait for the teacher to explain stuff I already know, and half of them don't even practice. They just don't get it."

I twirled my spaghetti around my fork. "Well, I'm glad that *you* get it," I replied. "And look at this way. You get to be the superstar in the class."

It was *great* for her self-esteem.

She gave me a conspiratorial smile. "That's true, actually. The teacher always gets me to demonstrate."

I held out my fist. "Pound it."

Just as we bumped knuckles, the telephone rang. I set down my fork to get up and answer it.

─⊙

"Carla," the voice said on the other end. "It's Officer Wallace. We met a few weeks ago when you were involved in a collision."

The authoritative sound of Officer Wallace's voice on the phone caught me off guard. Why was he calling? Was there a problem? Because I sometimes did feel it was "criminal," driving around in a gorgeous new Toyota Corolla.

I cleared my throat and tried to sound professional. "Yes, I remember you. Hello."

"I'm calling to follow up and see how you're doing," he said. "Did your insurance come through okay?"

I cleared my throat again. "Yes. I have a new car now but I'm being very careful. I learned my lesson."

There was a pause on the other end of the line, then I was quite sure I heard him chuckle.

"I'm glad to hear it," he said. "But I was lying to you just now. That's not really why I'm calling."

I glanced back at the table. Kaleigh had just finished her spaghetti and was carrying her plate to the dishwasher.

There was another pause. "I have a question to ask you," he said, "and I'm not really sure if it's appropriate."

"Um…" I had no idea what to say.

I was glad when Kaleigh left the kitchen to go practice her guitar in her room.

"That sounds really bad, doesn't it?" he added. "I knew I was going to mess this up."

Sensing his unease, I couldn't help but laugh. "I think you're going to have to spit it out, officer."

"It's Josh, remember?" he said. "And I'm calling to see if you're free this weekend."

Realizing that this had nothing to do with my collision—that it was very much a personal call—I leaned back against the counter and grinned.

"That depends," I replied. "I'm afraid I'm going to need to know why you're asking."

I could just picture him, pacing around his living room, wondering what to say.

"Well, you see," he hesitantly said, "I have this wedding to go to this weekend, and I need a date."

"Who's getting married?" I asked.

"My mom."

"Your mom! You're kind of leaving this to the last minute aren't you?"

He chuckled again. "I've been busy."

"Busy filling out traffic reports about female drivers who aren't paying close enough attention to the road?"

"Pretty much."

I laughed again. "Your mom's really getting married this weekend?"

"Yeah. She's marrying the man she met twenty years ago after she split up with my dad. He's pretty much been my step-dad all this time, but now he wants to make an honest woman out of her. It'll just be a small gathering. About thirty people, casual reception afterward. No head table or anything like that. But they're having it catered so there will be food and a cake."

"Sounds cozy and intimate," I replied. "Are you sure your mom would be okay with it?"

"Yeah, I already told her about you. She's a bit of a news junkie and she followed the story about your husband's plane crash. She asked me to pass on her condolences."

"Thank you. That's very kind," I replied.

We were both quiet for a few seconds. I picked up the dish-cloth and wiped the countertop.

"So will you come?" Josh asked.

I thought about how I'd been chiding myself lately for not getting out there and meeting interesting men.

"What time?" I asked.

"The ceremony starts at six," he said, "but I have to be there early because I'm walking her down the aisle."

"That's so nice. But are you absolutely sure you want to bring me? I'm a complete stranger."

"Nobody's a stranger to my mom," he replied. "Please say yes, and I'll pick you up at five."

More than a little aware that I was hemming and hawing, I shut my eyes and forced myself to respond. "Okay. It sounds like fun."

"It will be. I promise," he replied.

We hung up and I felt a flutter of excitement in my belly. Immediately I went to my closet to see what I might have to wear. There wasn't much, unfortunately, so I picked up the phone and called Audrey.

"Wow," Josh said when he stepped out of his car and watched me approach. "You look incredible."

"You don't look so shabby yourself," I replied, crossing the sidewalk to where he was parked at the curb just outside my building.

Audrey had lent me a cute little lime-green dress with a narrow black belt. I wore it with my patent leather spike heels and my hair swept into a loose twist.

This was the first time I'd seen Josh since he drove Kaleigh and me to the hospital after my collision. On that day, he was wearing his black officer's uniform, hat and gun belt. Tonight he wore a sharply tailored black suit with a crimson tie and polished black shoes.

I had to admit, he was one wickedly handsome man, and my heart did a little jump in my chest.

He came around and opened my door for me, then circled back to the driver's side. Soon we were on our way, and I couldn't help but give him a curious look.

"I find it hard to believe you didn't already have a date lined up for this," I said.

"Maybe I didn't *want* to bring a date," he said.

I narrowed my gaze at him. "Then what am I doing here? You're not going to try and fix me up with your great Uncle Henry or something, are you?"

He laughed. "Not a chance. You're all mine tonight."

"Hah! Don't be so sure about *that*," I replied with a chuckle. "Let's just see how the first hour goes."

As we drove through the city, I worked through the math... How long had it been since a handsome man flirted so openly with me?

Or maybe overtures had been made over the years. I just hadn't noticed because I'd always considered myself to be a married woman.

It was in that moment I looked down at my hands and realized I was still wearing my wedding ring. Discreetly, I covered my ring finger with my purse and marveled at the fact that I was sitting in a sleek Mazda6 on a Saturday night—driving to a wedding with a seriously hot cop who was about to walk his mother down the aisle.

Life certainly was full of surprises.

We arrived at the church about a half hour before the ceremony was set to begin, and Josh introduced me to his sister Marie, her husband Kevin and their three children who were all under the age of ten.

Marie and Kevin invited me to sit with them in one of the front pews where we became better acquainted and I learned all sorts of juicy details about Josh. Marie went on and on about him, gushing non-stop, saying things like 'I can't believe he's still single when he's so good looking, and he's such a great guy. Just wait until you get to know him better. All he ever wanted was to get married and have a house full of kids. It boggles my mind that it hasn't happened by now.'

"Why hasn't it?" I asked, glancing back at him in the entrance to the church where we was greeting guests. I wondered what the problem was.

"Because he got burned by a horrid monster of a woman who cheated on him with his best friend. It completely destroyed him. You're the first girl he's shown an interest in…" She nudged Kevin. "How long has it been since the Brooke disaster?"

"Almost two years," Kevin replied.

My head drew back. "Two years. Really. That long?"

Marie nodded and grinned. "Yes, so you can imagine how happy we are to meet *you*."

Clearly there were some lofty expectations here tonight. What had Josh told them about me?

"The truth is, we only just met," I mentioned. "It was a couple of weeks ago when I stupidly drove through a red light."

"He told us everything," Marie replied, leaning in to touch my knee. "And no pressure," she whispered. "I'm just glad he's finally getting out there, you know?"

"Hey, I know what it's like," I said. "I've been burned a few times myself. It's not always easy to get back on a bucking horse that's already kicked you in the face a few times."

The organist began to play the wedding march, and we all stood up to watch Josh walk his mother down the aisle.

"*arla*," Josh's mother said with warm affection as I moved through the reception line. She pulled me into her arms and hugged me. "I'm so glad you could come."

"Congratulations," I replied. "It's nice to meet you. The ceremony was beautiful."

"Thank you. You are an angel to say so."

I moved along the line to shake hands with her new husband—a tall slender man with thinning hair and glasses.

"You're a good sport," Josh said with a laugh when I reached him in the receiving line.

We stood for a long moment, smiling at each other, shaking hands, not letting go.

"Your family is very hospitable," I mentioned. "I'm having a good time so far."

"I'm glad," he replied. "Save me a dance later?"

"A dance? My word. I didn't know there would be *dancing*."

Slowly and smoothly, I pulled my hand from his.

"We Wallaces know how to throw a party," he told me. "I hope you like champagne."

"Doesn't everyone?"

His brown eyes glimmered in the setting sun. "I'll see you in a few minutes. The reception's not far from here. We'll drive over together."

"Okay." I strolled casually across the church parking lot toward his car and tried to remember the last time I'd felt butterflies like these.

Good golly, it might have been high school.

～∽

There's no point dragging this out or playing coy. By the time Josh met me at his car—after approaching with a masculine swagger that made my knees go weak—I was smitten.

The fact that he was tall, dark, muscular and handsome played a big role in my precipitous infatuation. Let's be honest. He was drop-dead gorgeous in a suit, not to mention his police officer's uniform. But there was so much more to it than that.

I was surprised by how moved I was by his amiable family, how devoted he was to them, and how I could relate to the fact that he was gun-shy in the romance department—because if anyone had a leg up on that, it was me.

I'd been through the wringer with Seth, not just during our confusing relationship when he could never truly commit to staying with Kaleigh and me. I'd also been crushed by the sudden loss of him. Though we had our problems, I did love him, and it hadn't been easy to attend his memorial service and say good-bye. He was Kaleigh's father after all.

"Ready to go?" Josh said as he pressed the button on the key remote to unlock the vehicle. He opened the car door for me and I smiled at him as I got in.

"It was a beautiful ceremony," I said.

"I sure hope so," he replied, "because they're both beautiful people. If anyone deserves to be happy, it's those two."

He shut my door and I sat in the passenger seat, feeling rather spellbound as I watched him outside, chatting and shaking hands with an older gentleman before getting into the driver's seat beside me.

"The reception's only a few blocks away," he said, "and we don't have to wait for the bride and groom to get through a two-hour photo shoot. Mom just wants candids taken at the inn. Are you hungry?"

"Not too bad," I replied as he backed out of the parking spot. "And thanks for inviting me to this."

He slid me a look. "Don't thank me just yet. You haven't met my Great-aunt Beatrice. She likes to pinch cheeks—*hard*—and she's got thumbs like a gorilla. I'm just sayin'."

"Thanks for the warning," I replied with a laugh.

But geez, he wasn't kidding. I discovered how serious he was the moment I met her.

The reception was held in an upscale Victorian inn not far from the church, and following cocktails, a hot meal was served in the dining room. Toasts were delivered and Josh gave a touching speech about his mom that made my eyes well up.

After dinner, a DJ played music in the large parlor and front hall where they rolled back the carpets for dancing on the hardwood floors.

I barely had a chance to sit down. I danced with Josh's uncles, his cousins, and with the children, too. His five-year-old niece, Susie, took a particular shine to me, and I spent some time upstairs in her room at the inn with Marie, where they showed me her dollhouse, which they'd brought from home.

By midnight the children were falling asleep on the lounge chairs in the parlor, and at one o'clock, the DJ announced the last dance.

Josh turned to me and held out his hand. "*Great* song."

A shiver of excitement rippled up my spine, because it had been a perfect night and this would be the perfect ending—to slow dance with Josh to Van Morrison's *Into the Mystic*, one of my all-time favorite songs.

Earlier, he had removed his suit jacket and loosened his tie, so I could feel the smooth muscular contours of his broad shoulders under the white shirt as I slid my hand up his arm.

"I hope you had a good time," he said, holding me close.

"It was great," I replied. "Your family's amazing."

Just then, Marie and Kevin tangoed over to us and said, "You guys hungry? 'Cuz we're going to order some pizzas after this."

"That sounds great," Josh said, "but I'm sure Carla wants to get home."

"No way!" Marie protested. "You can't drive her anyway. I saw how much champagne you had, little brother. Why don't you stay, Carla?" she said to me.

My eyebrows lifted. "Stay?"

"Yes, we have the whole inn booked just for our family. Half the rooms are empty. You can choose any one you want and have breakfast with us in the morning and stay to watch Mom and Eric open their gifts."

"I wouldn't want to impose," I said.

"You wouldn't be. Unless you have to get home to your daughter…?"

"She's spending the night with her cousin," I explained.

"Well, there you have it," Marie said. "It's decided. You have to stay."

I turned my eyes to Josh to try and get a reading on how he might feel about that.

"Stay," he said with encouragement. "I'd like to spend some more time with you."

Maybe it was too much too soon, and maybe I should have known better because that's how I'd gotten myself in trouble in the past—by not looking before I leaped. It's how I ended up married to a man who didn't really want to be married.

But the fact remained that lately I'd swung too far in the opposite direction and had been playing it safe for too long. This was the best night I'd had in ages and I didn't want it to end.

Besides, what harm could come of it? It was only one night and I'd have my own room.

After we finished eating the pizza, Josh and I took our wine glasses and retreated to the small private sunroom at the back of the inn. It was lit by a single kerosene lamp and decorated with floral fabrics. We sat on a wicker love seat with a chintz cushion and looked out at the gently falling snow in the dark yard.

"Do you realize this is the first time we've been alone together all night?" Josh asked as he rested his arm along the back of the seat.

"You noticed too?" Clearly there was an intense undercurrent of attraction between us that I found both exhilarating and nerve-racking. "I had a nice time," I said. "I really needed this."

He nodded in agreement. "You had a rough year."

"From what I heard, you haven't had such a great year yourself," I casually mentioned. Then I waved a hand and shook my head. "I'm sorry. Marie was eager to share all the details of your personal life with me."

The corner of his mouth curved up in a grin and he leaned forward to set his wine glass down on the coffee table.

"My sister was never very good at keeping secrets," he said with affection, "which wasn't exactly her best quality in high school, because somehow Mom and Eric always found out about any wild parties that were going on and arrived promptly at midnight to drag me home."

"Sounds like you owe your sister a debt of gratitude for keeping you on the straight and narrow."

He nodded. "I know it. And I'm not sorry she told you about my past either. It saves me from having to explain it myself, because *that's* never awkward."

I smiled.

"Now that it's out in the open, we have no secrets," Josh added.

I rested my temple on a finger. "What a pair we are. Between the two of us, we have enough baggage to fill a small backyard shed."

Josh agreed and reached for my hand. "And you still wear this," he said, rubbing the pad of his thumb over my wedding ring.

While his gaze was lowered, I took the opportunity to study the strong features of his face—his dark eyelashes, the straight nose, the full lips and perfectly sculpted cheekbones and jawline.

"I hadn't really thought about it until tonight," I said, glancing down at my ring again, "when we were in the car after the ceremony. Maybe I should have taken it off by now, but I'm just so used to wearing it."

His eyes lifted and met mine. "You'll know when the time is right. No need to rush it."

"I think a part of me likes the fact that it sends a message and prevents guys from asking me out. If they look at my hand and see that I'm married, they move on."

"Except for me," he said with an intense look. "I didn't move on. Was that wrong?"

"No," I replied. "I'm glad you called."

He picked up his wine glass and took a sip. "So tell me about Seth. If he was a professional climber, he must have been gone quite a bit."

I rolled my eyes. "You don't know the half of it." Then I stopped talking for a moment and looked down at my hands. "If you really want to know the truth, I don't think he ever wanted to be married. He just felt obligated because we had a child together." I explained.

"Ah," Josh replied.

I shrugged. "It's been hard for me to keep that from Kaleigh. I don't want her to ever feel like she caused me to choose something I wouldn't have chosen otherwise."

"But *would* you have chosen it?" Josh asked. "If you hadn't had Kaleigh, do you think you would have eventually ended up married to Seth anyway?"

"Do you want me to be completely honest?" I asked.

He nodded.

I let out a sigh. "It's not easy to say this. It feels disrespectful because he's gone now, but looking back on it, realistically, I'm quite sure our relationship would have fizzled before it came anywhere close to marriage. Not because *I* didn't want it. I was young and foolish and madly in love, and the fact that he was so elusive, you know, unavailable to me…He was always talking about leaving for the next big climb. That just made me want to hang on to him tighter. It was like he was playing hard to get and it worked like a charm on me. Though of course it wasn't intentional on his part. He really was genuinely out of reach. Impossible to pin down." I paused and looked out the window.

"I was so young. I didn't have enough life experience. I was following my heart, not my head. Although now that I think about it, it wasn't really my heart. It was probably mostly my

ego. I felt like I was competing with the mountain for his atten-
tions—Everest in particular—and I wanted to be the one to win.
I figured if I was just patient enough, and supportive enough,
he'd get tired of that life and want to come home."

"Sounds like you were very patient," Josh said.

"Yes, but sadly, in the end, none of us really won, except maybe
the mountain because it's still there, doing its thing. Seriously…
Everest was the 'other woman' in our relationship. Then it was K2."

Josh set down his wine glass and I glanced out the window
again.

"It looks cold out there," I said. "I do love the outdoors as
much as the next person, but on a night like this, I'm glad to be
inside."

Marie knocked on the door jamb and peeked her head into
the sunroom. "I have your room key," she said to me.

"Great, thank you."

She walked in and handed it to me.

I turned it over in my hand. "Wow—a real old-fashioned
brass key, not a plastic card."

"This is a classy joint," Marie said. "You're in room 307. It
has a canopy bed and a tiny private balcony under one of the
dormers."

"That sounds lovely. Thank you so much."

"I also told the front desk to send up a toothbrush and toothpaste, and there's a bathrobe in the room so you should be all set."
Marie turned to go.

"Are you going to bed, sis?" Josh asked, and I noticed it had
grown quiet in the front rooms of the inn.

"Yes," Marie replied. "Mom and Eric just went up to their
suite and the kids are down for the count. We'll see you two in
the morning." She left us alone again.

I slipped the key into my purse and leaned back on the love seat. "What room are *you* in?" I asked Josh.

"309," he replied. "Do you think she planned that?"

I laughed. "Probably."

We both smiled, slouched down next to each other and put our feet up on the coffee table.

Josh and I stayed up talking until the wee hours of the morning. We talked about our past relationships and he told me about how the woman he'd imagined himself marrying had had a few too many drinks one night and slept with his best friend from college who had come to visit for the weekend.

Josh was no longer in touch with either of them.

When I started yawning, we decided it was time to call it a night. Josh turned down the dimmer in the sunroom lamp. Quietly we moved through the dark, wood-paneled inn and climbed the stairs.

"We didn't talk about your job," I whispered to Josh. I was sleepy but not yet ready to say goodnight. "I wanted to ask what made you want to become a cop."

Slowly, taking one step at a time, he told me how, at the age of sixteen, he had been home one night babysitting his younger brothers and sisters. Unexpectedly, their next door neighbor came outside with a rifle and began screaming at his wife, who was still inside. Then he fired shots at the house.

"We were all in shock," Josh whispered as we reached the second floor and continued up the stairs. "I didn't know what to do at first, then I sent the others down to the basement and told them to lock themselves in the bathroom. I called the police and waited at the window until I saw them pull up in a blaze of sirens and flashing lights. The cops got out of their vehicles and started yelling at our neighbor to drop his weapon. Thankfully he complied and they stormed onto his front lawn. They had him sprawled in the grass and were cuffing him within seconds. Then they came to my door and asked me all sorts of questions and congratulated me for making the call, told me I did the right thing…And that's the moment I knew what I wanted to be."

By now we had reached the third floor and he was walking me down the corridor to my room.

"That's quite a story," I said. "Have you had many calls like that yourself?"

We reached room 307, but stopped just outside. Josh faced me and leaned a shoulder against the wall.

"Too many to count. Lots of times I glance back and see civilians looking out their windows at us when we're taking someone into custody, and they always have that same wide-eyed expression, like they can't believe what they just witnessed. I remember feeling that way in my front window that night. I was never so happy to see those flashing lights come around the corner, because I was terrified our neighbor was going to turn around and start shooting at us, too."

"Are you terrified now, when you have to answer a call like that?" I asked.

"Not terrified," he replied, speaking softly. "But adrenaline kicks in sometimes."

For a long moment we stood outside my room, neither of us making a move to say goodnight, and the mention of adrenaline made me realize I had a mad flock of butterflies in my belly. Feeling suddenly frazzled, I dug into my purse for the room key.

"Guess it's time for bed," I said as I withdrew it.

Josh pushed away from the wall and gave me a heated look that set my blood on fire.

"Goodnight, Carla," he said, his voice husky and low as he leaned in and kissed me on the cheek. "I'll see you in the morning."

With that, he turned away and all I could do was stand there in a dazed stupor, watching him dig into his pocket for his own key and smile at me one more time before disappearing into his room.

What a gentleman, I thought, as I closed my door behind me. How wonderful to know they still existed.

Circles

Aaron

I realize it might seem implausible that one man could live through a plane crash, a lynx attack, and be chased by a polar bear in one lifetime. And that wasn't even all.

When I was somewhat recovered from my flight from the bear and my violent tumble down the mountain, I gathered up my belongings and continued to walk along the coast, hoping to eventually reach civilization.

To make a long story short, after about a week of constant walking, I found myself back in the same spot where I'd been chased by the bear, and my heart sank as low as it had ever been.

How was this even possible? True, I'd neglected to use the compass because I didn't see it as a necessity if I was traveling along the coastline. But here I stood again, overlooking the same the beach, the same walruses, the same rocky cliff I'd jumped over to save myself from a mauling.

That was the day I realized I was not in the Canadian province of Newfoundland, but rather I was stranded on an uninhabited island somewhere in the middle of the North Atlantic and I had walked a full circle around it.

I can't even describe the level of my frustration. All I could do was shrug out of my backpack, drop it on the ground and roar a terrible obscenity at the sky. I picked up snowballs and pitched them across the beach at the water. I shouted expletives and kicked my backpack repeatedly.

It's a good thing the bear wasn't nearby listening for supper possibilities. Or maybe he was, and I scared him away.

—⟡—

Summer on the island spun in and out all too quickly. Thankfully it provided me with a much needed respite from the chill of the merciless wind blowing across those rugged, desolate winter landscapes.

To my delight, a great diversity of plants and flowers bloomed on the limestone coastal barrens, breaking through the cracks in the rocks, creating colorful natural crevice gardens. Day after day, I walked along the cliffs on sunny, breezy afternoons, feasting upon scarlet-colored edible berries and picking flowers to take back to my dark cave—a place where I had established a more permanent residence after the tent fell apart in a windstorm.

In the forests, stunted birch and maple trees grew lush with leaves, then turned red and gold as autumn rolled in.

By then I had at least learned to snare rabbits and catch fish with an expert efficiency, and somehow I managed not to go completely stark-raving mad at the mere notion of spending another winter on the island.

Stay alive, I told myself each night in the cave as I sat before the fire, staring into the flames and then glancing across at the only picture I had of another human being.

So beautiful…

Stay alive, Aaron, just one more day.

Stay alive.

Desperation

Winter swept in again like a vengeful beast.

For many months, I survived on fish, kelp and rabbit meat, and even on that diet had been reduced to probably two-thirds of my body weight.

Mentally, for my self-preservation, I retreated into my cave and also into a world of fantasy where I entertained myself with dreams of another life. That, at least, gave me something to live for—the dream of returning home.

To my loved ones. Television, restaurants, coffee grinders, cars and books. My guitar.

Sometimes I would sit on a log and stare at trees for hours, picturing these things in elaborate detail. I heard them. Smelled them. Replayed memories in my mind. I often strummed guitar chords in my head.

Weddings…When was the last time I'd sat in a church?

Music. *Oh, God…music.*

The sound of a lawn mower. The smell of cut grass.

Carla's blue eyes.

All these images helped to fill my empty, lonely days, until I woke up one morning and realized it had been more than a year since I'd boarded the plane and crashed into this God-forsaken place.

That's when something took hold of me—a pressing, desperate need to go home, and something about it felt like my last chance. Somehow I knew that if I didn't go now, with spring on the horizon, all would be lost.

I had turned forty on this lonesome rock and my life was slipping away.

Did anyone miss me? My parents and sister—most assuredly. But I had no wife, no children.

I thought of how I'd always wanted a son.

Nothing but a pipe dream now.

Perhaps that's what did it. That's what set me off—the unlikelihood that I would ever achieve any of these things, and a sense of powerlessness that drove me almost mad with despair and longing.

Consequently, I woke up one morning after a light snowfall and returned to the ridge where I first saw the ocean and walruses and the polar bear.

Exhausted and out of breath from the hike, I collapsed in the snow and lay for a long time, staring up at the clear blue sky. A cloud hovered up there, directly over my head. It looked like an X. Then it rotated and became a cross. Then it spun and turned into an X again.

It was quiet on the ridge, except for the gentle rhythmic swish of the waves washing the rocky beach below. Maybe I would encounter the polar bear again. Would he remember me?

Weak and tired, I rolled onto my hands and knees, paused for a few seconds, then rose to my feet.

There, before me, lay the flat, silvery sea dappled with shining white icebergs drifting south in the distance. I stared at them, mesmerized, while listening to the sound of the waves.

Striding forward, curious to know if the walruses were out, I briefly took my gaze off the horizon—until something totally unexpected caught my attention and my eyes grew wide.

A pair of binoculars would have come in handy, but all I had were my own two weary, bloodshot eyeballs.

Squinting tightly, I strained to focus on what I thought I saw in the distance. *Could it be? Or was I dreaming again?*

I strode faster, all the way to the edge of the cliff and shaded my eyes with my gloved hand.

There. Yes.

It wasn't an iceberg or a whale. Sweet Mother of God, it was a ship. A tiny speck in the distance, but a huge container ship, most likely.

I began to jump up and down, waving my arms frantically over my head. *"Hey! Over here! I'm here! This way!"*

But the ship continued on—its gradual movement barely discernible on the faraway horizon.

I squatted down on my haunches, sat there in quiet awe, and watched it until it was completely out of sight.

Over the next five days, I returned at dawn to the same spot on the ridge and sat quietly all day next to a signal fire, watching the horizon. Whales and porpoises swam by, and icebergs drifted in peaceful, communal silence. Everything was crisp and blue, and soon my head ached from the strain on my eyes.

With each passing day, I grew a little less hopeful.

On the sixth day, however, I saw something new, something out of the ordinary, and shot up from my squatting position on the snow.

Using both gloved hands, I shaded my eyes from the sun and pulled my eyebrows together to squint further into the distance.

There! Yes! Again! I hadn't been dreaming! It was another container ship!

I threw more branches on the fire, and like before, jumped up and down and waved my arms over my head, despite the fact that I knew it was futile. They were too far away, and I was a fool to be shouting in polar bear territory.

So I quickly squatted down again and like before, watched the ship in silence until it disappeared from view.

While sitting there, however, I began to formulate a plan.

Twenty-one days after I spotted that first ship on the horizon and came to the realization that I was not far from a transatlantic shipping lane, I had built myself a raft and was ready to depart.

I gave no thought to polar bears as I dragged my vessel onto the windy beach, pushed it into the frigid North Atlantic waters and hopped on.

I had spent many hours chopping down trees and lashing the trunks together with long twisted strips of the nylon fabric I'd saved from the tent. I even used a section of the plane to create a waterproof floor with raised edges.

I had collected icicles—chipped them into small bits and stored them in the little booze bottles I'd found when I returned to the plane.

I also armed myself with fishing lines and hooks—from the dried bones of rabbits—and by this point I was blindly determined to push away from the beach and leave here forever.

The walruses didn't seem to care that I was going. None of them so much as lifted their heads to watch.

As I bobbed up and down on the swells and began to float out to where the icebergs and whales made their home, I looked back and wondered if the island would miss me. It had been my home for a full year and I'd most certainly left my mark on it.

I thought of the lynx staring at me in the darkness. Seth standing on the edge of the mountain, then slipping from view. I remembered my tears on that day.

Then I thought of the angry white bear that had roared at me on the beach.

No, I would not miss this island. As I floated away in the cold, blustery wind and felt the salty stinging spray on my cheeks, I decided that come what may—I would rather take my chances with the sea than remain here for another year.

Though it was undoubtedly a risky undertaking, in my defense, I did not leave the island without a plan. I had consulted my compass and established a field bearing when I spotted the ships, and I knew exactly which direction I had to paddle.

I'd packed enough food and water to last a week, and was prepared to catch more fish if necessary. I had an A-frame shelter I had constructed from an evergreen sapling and some boughs, and I'd also fashioned four serviceable oars——two as backups——and had been alternatively rowing and drifting towards the area where I believed I would eventually cross paths with a ship.

Little did I know that the sea—just like the island—would not welcome me either. Again, I was in foreign territory and unfortunately for me, there would be challenges ahead.

All I had on my side was luck—which I suppose is what I'd had in spades from the beginning, though I didn't always see it that way.

O n my second day on the water, late in the afternoon, I felt
something bump up against the bottom of my raft.
Instantly alert, I crawled out of my shelter where I'd been
resting.

The sky was overcast and there wasn't a whisper of wind. The
water was calm and gray and I was floating between bergs and
small slabs of ice.

I wondered if I'd knocked into one of them.

A gentle but chilly breeze caressed my face. The salty fra-
grance of the sea filled my nostrils while water lapped gently
against the sides of my craft.

Thump.

My eyes flew open and I lost my balance, fell onto my
backside.

What was that?

Curious, I looked over the side. A black and white shadow
moved beneath the surface. Then another shadow slid by, and
another.

Perched on all fours, I gazed from left to right to scan the
shiny flat surface of the water around me.

A black fin rose out of the depths about ten yards away and
dove down again.

Killer whales.

Just then, a large face bobbed out of the water like a cork directly beside me. Startled out of my wits, I scrambled back into my shelter. "Holy crap!"

Another whale bobbed his head up out of the water, as if to determine exactly who, and what, I was.

There must have been five of them, large and small, swimming beneath me in circles. Maybe they were just curious, or playing.

Then, from a greater distance, two of them, side by side, swam like a couple of torpedoes toward me.

With wide eyes I watched them approach and braced myself as they rose to the surface a few yards away, then dove down under my vessel, sweeping me up on a wave they'd created.

Thwack!

My raft collided with something and nearly knocked me onto my back. Swinging around, I found myself staring up at a giant iceberg, close enough to touch.

To keep my balance, I grabbed hold of my A-frame shelter which was lashed tightly around my makeshift deck, then looked down and saw that the waterproof floor under my feet had cracked right down the center. Water was already sloshing around my boots, and I knew that if I sank into the icy water, I would be dead within minutes. Even if the raft remained afloat, I wouldn't survive long if I was wet.

A young whale bobbed his head out of the water and looked at me. He almost appeared to be smiling or laughing. Then the two older whales circled around and joined forces again from a distance away.

What were they up to? As far as I knew, orcas were supposed to be friendly mammals, and I'd heard there were no cases of attacks on humans ever recorded in the wild. Was I to be the first? Or did they mistake me for a seal? Maybe no one had lived to tell the tale…

Together, they swam in my direction again, picking up speed, just like before, and by doing so, they created another wave that swept my raft right up onto a flat section of the iceberg.

Feeling threatened by these giant creatures—not knowing their minds or their intent—and without taking time to think about it, I hopped off my broken raft and scrambled up to where the ice was dry. For many minutes I stood there motionless, staring.

The whales continued to frolic, and created another wave that splashed up onto the berg. Suddenly, my raft was taken away, along with my backpack and all my food and supplies.

"No!" I shouted, lurching forward to try and catch it, but the waves were still crashing up onto the ice. I had to scramble backwards or risk getting washed away as well.

Oh, Lord, what had I done? Why hadn't I tried to secure it? All I could do was watch in horror as it floated farther and farther away.

Then, to my surprise, water seeped up through the cracks in the floor of my raft, filling it like a bowl, and it sank into the sea.

Oh, My God…

The next thing I knew I was half way up the slope of ice, using both axes from my belt to help me climb.

I wasn't wearing crampons, so I have no idea how I made it to the top. Superhuman strength fueled by fear, perhaps?

By nightfall I was sitting on top of the iceberg, which was as tall as a three-story building. Hugging my knees to my chest, I watched the sun set over the horizon.

All my belongings were gone. My raft had sunk and I had no food.

At least now I was surrounded by an unlimited supply of fresh water—because that's what icebergs were made of. All I had to do was chip away at my floating island any time I felt thirsty.

But how long could I go without food and warmth?

Food…

Maybe five days? At most, a week.

Warmth?

Not nearly that long.

So there it was.

My fate was sealed. Survival was out of my hands now, for all I had in my possession was what I carried in my pockets and the two axes hooked on the belt of Seth's old jacket.

I took a deep breath, then slowly, achingly, I let go of myself, lay back and stretched out on the ice to look up at the stars.

Billions of them.

What a night. So clear and magically celestial under a gigantic full moon while its light glistened on the surface of the calm water below.

It was so impossibly beautiful, it moved me to tears.

God, if you can hear me, I give up. If you want to take me now, you can, and if this was your plan all along, I'm sorry for fighting so hard against you. I just really wanted to go home.

How quiet it was on top of the iceberg. I never knew such silence.

And so I surrendered to the situation and I floated.

The sun went down, I closed my eyes, and I floated. Far, far away.

Contact

Carla

I should have known it would be a strange night when the power went out mere seconds before the telephone rang.

Kaleigh was in her bedroom practicing her guitar and I was sitting on the sofa watching a repeat episode of *How I Met Your Mother*. Suddenly everything went black and the TV went *pop* before shutting down.

Kaleigh called out to me. "*Mom!*"

"It's just the power!" I called back. "I'm getting a flashlight!"

Her door flew open. "Where are you?"

"I'm in the living room," I replied in a calm voice as I felt my way along the wall toward the junk drawer in the kitchen.

I pulled it open, dug around until I found the flashlight, turned it on and handed it to Kaleigh. "Here, use this." Then I crossed the kitchen to answer the phone. "Hello?"

"Hello, is this Carla Matthews?"

The voice on the other end sounded far away, as if it was a bad connection.

"Yes, this is she."

There was a brief pause. "Hi. My name is Donna Fisher and I'm a nurse calling from St. Agnes Hospital in Newfoundland, Canada. Are you the wife of Seth Jameson?"

My chest constricted with panic and dread. Instinctively, I turned my back on Kaleigh, wanting to shield her from whatever news was about to befall us—at least until I had a chance to deal with it myself.

"Yes, that's me," I replied.

Another pause. "Well…I have good news and not so good news," she said. "The good news is that a man was brought into the hospital this afternoon and we believe he might be your missing husband."

Her words reverberated inside my brain and I couldn't breathe for a moment. *"What?"*

"He was discovered this morning on top of an iceberg," Donna continued, "floating in the ocean north of here, but we have no idea how he came to be there. He was spotted by a crew member on a container ship passing through the area, and it's a miracle they saw him. They had quite a time getting to him."

"Oh, My God," I replied, laying a hand on my chest and turning to face Kaleigh who was staring at me with wide eyes.

"He was rescued and brought in by helicopter," Donna explained, "but I have to warn you, he's not doing so well. We have no idea how long he was out there. He was unresponsive when they reached him and he hasn't regained consciousness."

I was having a hard time comprehending all of this. I didn't know what to do. "But he's alive?" I asked.

"Yes, but severely hypothermic and malnourished. We understand he was involved in a plane crash a year ago?"

"That's right."

She paused again. "I can't believe he survived all this time. It truly is a miracle."

There was that word again.

I felt Kaleigh's hand on my arm. "What is it, Mom?" she asked. "What's happening?"

I held her tightly in my gaze. My heart felt like it was going to explode. "It's unbelievable. They found your father."

In that moment, the lights came back on.

As soon as I hung up the phone and explained the particulars to Kaleigh, I immediately called Gladys and told her everything I knew.

She wept uncontrollably and asked when Seth would be able to come home. I told her they didn't want to move him yet. She asked if I would travel to Newfoundland.

"Of course I'm going," I replied, feeling a sense of urgency that made me want to run out the door that very second. "As soon as we hang up I'll see about booking a flight first thing in the morning."

"I want to go with you," she said. "I need to see him."

I hesitated. "I understand, but you'll have to prepare yourself. It won't be easy. He's not conscious and they said he looks like a mountain man—he's quite emaciated. Almost unrecognizable. I'm sure they'll have him cleaned up by the time we get there, but it'll be difficult to see him like that, Gladys."

I couldn't bear the thought of it myself. Every time I imagined what he must have gone through, tears filled my eyes and my legs turned to jelly.

"I don't care," she sobbed. "I just want to hold my son's hand."

"Me, too," I replied. Then I reached for a tissue and wiped my eyes. "But we have to be strong. This is good news. We should hang up so I can get us booked on a flight. I'll call you back as soon as I have things worked out. Stay by the phone."

"I will," she replied.

I ended the call and turned to meet Kaleigh's intense gaze. "Can I come?" she asked.

This was not an easy moment. I wasn't sure if my twelve-year-old daughter could handle it.

What if Seth doesn't survive? I thought. *What if, by the time we get there, he is already gone?*

A terrible heaviness settled into my heart.

"Yes, you can come," I replied even though I worried about what we might have to endure. I held out my arms and pulled her into my embrace.

—⟶

It didn't take long for me to go online and book three early morning flights out of Boston. I did this without even asking for time off at the bank and had to call my supervisor immediately afterward. Thank heavens she was understanding and told me to take all the time I needed.

It was not until I went into my room to pack a bag that I realized I hadn't spoken to Josh yet.

My stomach rolled over with uncertainty and I sank onto the edge of my bed. For a long while I sat with my hand over my mouth.

Josh and I had been seeing each other for almost three months now, and things were getting serious. I adored his family, and they adored me, and I'd even gone so far as to introduce him to Kaleigh.

Kaleigh liked him well enough and didn't openly object to my dating him, but she was sometimes withdrawn around him, which I supposed wasn't unusual for a girl her age. She'd often retreat into her room to play guitar and listen to music when he came over.

But Dear Lord, how was I supposed to handle this? Seth was my husband—Kaleigh's biological father—and I couldn't imagine what he had endured over the past year.

The nurse told me that all he had in his possession besides the clothes on his back were two climbing axes, a journal, his compass and wallet, which included a dog-eared picture of me.

"It was probably what kept him going all that time," she had said. "You were his angel."

I leaned forward on the bed and covered my face with both hands. *Oh, God, Seth. I'm so sorry.*

But sorry for what, exactly?

For everything he'd been through? For accepting that he was dead when he wasn't? For letting them call off the search too soon?

Or was I sorry for falling in love with another man?

I checked in on Kaleigh and found her lying on her bed listening to music with her ear buds in, so I decided it was as good a time as any to call Josh.

"Hey," he said, answering right away. "Great timing. I just finished my shift."

"Are you still at the station?" I asked, inching back against the headboard of my bed.

"Yeah, but I'm getting in my car to head home." The remote car door lock beeped and I heard the sound of the door opening and closing. "What's up?"

Relieved that he was alone, I gave him a moment to settle in. "I have some news and it's pretty big," I said. "Are you sitting down?"

"I am," he replied. "Should I buckle in?"

"Maybe. Gosh, I don't even know where to begin." I took a deep breath and let it out. "A little while ago I received a phone call from a nurse in a hospital in Newfoundland, Canada. She said they found a man floating on an iceberg in the middle of the ocean and they're pretty sure it's Seth."

"Oh my God," Josh said. "On an iceberg? How is that even possible? Is he alive?"

"Barely," I replied. "She said he was unresponsive when they got to him and he hasn't regained consciousness. He's on life support."

"I'm so sorry," Josh said. "Jesus. Is there a prognosis? Do they know if he'll make it?"

"They couldn't say. It's very much touch and go. She suggested that we pray. A lot."

"Of course we will," Josh said. "But I can't believe it. It's been over a year. How did he survive all that time?"

"If anyone could survive in the north, it would be Seth," I replied. "Don't forget, he climbed Everest five times."

"The guy must be super human."

"I don't know about that," I said with a sigh. "You'd think someone who was super human would be able to do it all, but he never could. Oh, God, I can't believe I just said that. Today of all days."

Josh spoke in a gentle tone. "Clearly the two of you still have some issues to work out."

Did we? I wondered uncertainly, because over the past year I'd finally felt like I'd accepted that we were completely done, that we were never meant to be man and wife—never true mates for life.

But now...

"What are you going to do?" Josh asked. "Will you go and see him?"

"I have to," I replied. "I'm his wife and he's going to need help. I can't just abandon him. Not after everything he's been through."

Neither of us said anything for a moment. Then at last Josh spoke.

"I don't want to lose you," he whispered into the phone.

I felt the warmth of his voice in my ear.

"I don't want to lose you either," I replied. "And I don't know what's going to happen. Maybe we'll get there and…" I couldn't finish the sentence.

"But you have to go," he said. "I understand, and I want you to know that I'm here for you, Carla. No matter what."

Relief poured through me and my eyes fell closed. "Thank you, Josh. You're an amazing man."

He asked what time my flight was leaving in the morning, wished me luck, and asked me to keep him posted. I promised I would. Then we hung up and I turned over onto my side and hugged the pillow under my head.

The sound of the phone ringing caused me to jump. I reached for the receiver on the bedside table and nearly knocked over the lamp. "Hello?"

"Hello, is this Carla Matthews?"

I wiped a hand over my face. "Yes."

"Are you the wife of Seth Jameson, the alpine climber who went missing last year after his plane went down?"

"Yes, who is this?"

"My name is Jennie Leblanc and I'm calling from CNN. We understand a man was found floating on an iceberg in the North Atlantic and they believe him to be your husband. Would you mind talking to us about that?"

I had nearly fallen asleep before the phone rang and hadn't quite grasped what was going on. "CNN?" I replied. "Do you know anything? Are they sure it's him?"

Strangely, in my desire for more information about Seth, I assumed they knew more than I did.

"That's why I'm calling," she said. "Will you be traveling to Newfoundland to reunite with your husband?"

I paused a moment to regroup. "Yes, I'm flying out first thing in the morning."

"How is he doing?" she asked. "Have the doctors told you anything?"

Again I hesitated. "I really don't know very much. You're not going to play this phone call on television, are you?"

"Not without your permission," she replied, "but we'd love to do a video interview with you if you're willing."

I shook my head. "No, I really can't. This has been very difficult and I just want to go and see my husband. Please respect our privacy."

"Of course, I understand," she replied. "Will you be suing George Atherton?"

I blinked a few times and shook my head as if to clear it. "I don't know. I really can't think about that right now. I just need to see Seth."

In the end, I had to cut Jennie off and hang up because she wouldn't stop asking questions. The phone rang again a moment later—this time the call display indicated it was a newspaper, so I unplugged the phone from the wall.

A half hour later, as I was throwing clothes into a suitcase, there was a knock at my apartment door. I jumped because it was eleven o'clock at night and I wasn't expecting anyone. *If this is another reporter...*

I hurried down the hall to look through the peep hole and felt a surge of relief to see Josh.

"What are you doing here?" I asked as I opened the door.

He stood in the corridor, still in uniform, a pained look in his eyes. "I couldn't let you leave without seeing you."

Opening the door wider, I stepped back, inviting him in. He entered and waited until I closed and locked it before pulling me into his arms and holding me close.

"I don't know the right things to say," he whispered, "because he's your husband and what happened to him was terrible. I feel badly—really I do—and I know you have to go to him, but I don't want you to. I want everything to stay the way it is."

I wrapped my arms around his shoulders and buried my face in his neck. "I don't know the right words to say either. I feel like my whole world has just been flipped upside down. I'm glad Seth's alive but it's all so complicated. I don't know what I'm supposed to do, what my responsibilities are. Is it my duty to stay with him?"

Josh held me away from him to look into my eyes. "I haven't known you very long," he said, "but I know you need to do the right thing, and that means going to him now. And I love you for that. Really, Carla. I'm in love with you. No matter what happens, nothing's going to change that. I'll wait forever if I have to, or I'll let you go if that's what you want. But that's not what *I* want. I'm selfish—I know it—but I have to say this to you. If I don't, it'll haunt me forever."

"Say what?" I pleaded.

He paused. "You told me it was over between the two of you long before Seth ever got on that plane. If that's true, I don't think you should have to sacrifice your future because of a misguided sense of duty. I want you do what you need to do, but then I want you to come back to me."

He pressed his lips to mine and backed me up against the wall. Overcome by a mixture of confusion and desire, I clung to him in the dimly lit hallway, kissing him fiercely while struggling with guilt and confusion, because I was another man's wife—a man who was in a hospital up north, fighting for his life, and I felt such a strong pull to be there.

"This is wrong," I whispered in Josh's ear. "We shouldn't be doing this. Not now. Not until I get everything figured out."

He nodded and squeezed me in his arms, then took a step back. "I'll wait," he said. "I'll be here until you tell me it's over between us, and you convince me it's what you really want."

My breaths came hard and fast as he moved to the door and unlocked it. He paused only briefly to look at me one last time before he walked out, strode down the hallway and stepped onto the elevator.

A short while later, when I was all finished packing, I found myself sitting on the edge of my bed, looking down at my left hand and running the pad of my thumb over the place where my wedding band used to be.

I considered whether or not I should put it back on. What was the right thing to do? Could I show up at Seth's bedside without it? Gladys certainly wouldn't appreciate that.

Maybe I should have acted with more self-interest, but I decided to dig it out of my jewelry box and slide it back on my finger.

The flight to Newfoundland was smooth but grueling because we had to turn off our cell phones, and when I did, it felt as if we'd lost contact with Seth all over again.

The minute we landed, I called the hospital to find out how he was doing and they said he was the same. He had not yet regained consciousness.

Then, to our surprise, we were practically accosted by reporters who followed us out of the airport, asking questions about Seth and the plane crash. We walked quickly, said "No comment" repeatedly as we hurried into a cab.

Kaleigh never failed to surprise me with her incredible maturity from the moment the initial phone call about Seth came in, to when we arrived at the hotel.

She was my rock during the trip, and I don't know what I would have done without her. She fetched me coffee when I was tired during our layover, and she played cards with Gladys, which helped keep my mother-in-law calm and distracted from the thought of her son lying in a hospital bed, barely alive and completely alone.

Kaleigh also helped Gladys with her luggage and made sure she had everything as we went through security.

"Thank you for taking such good care of Gram," I whispered in her ear as we climbed out of the cab to check in at the hotel. "You've been a great help."

"I'm just glad to be here," she replied, "because he's my dad. I need to see him."

I felt another twinge of guilt when I met her gaze, because she knew how I felt about Josh and that I hadn't exactly been faithful to my missing husband over the past three months.

At the same time, I suspected she carried her own little purse of guilt for not feeling more grief initially when his plane went down. The truth of the matter was, Kaleigh had never felt a strong connection to Seth, though she'd wanted to. She'd wanted it quite desperately, and part of me believed she blamed herself for his lack of interest in being a real father to her.

Maybe there was hope that she might get what she so deeply desired. If Seth came through this with a new perspective on life, maybe he would finally be ready to become the father she'd always wanted.

But there I went again—always imagining that Seth might change and become the man we both wanted him to be. I'd been through this before, after K2.

But something felt different this time. It felt like the promise of a new beginning. Even if it meant saying good-bye.

As soon as we stepped off the elevator at the intensive care unit, my heart began to race. I noticed the familiar hospital smells of antiseptic and rubbing alcohol. They reminded me of my difficult labor and breach delivery with Kaleigh, when Seth was nowhere to be found.

As I scanned the area for the nurses' station, I said to Gladys. "It's this way." I couldn't begin to imagine what she must be feeling. Seth was her beloved son, miraculously back from the dead, but not quite back…

One of the nurses, who was seated behind the counter, immediately looked up from her computer screen when I told them who we were.

"I'm Donna," she said. "I spoke to you on the phone last night. You must be Carla?"

"Yes," I replied, "and this is Gladys, Seth's mother, and Kaleigh, our daughter."

"It's nice to meet you all," she said. "I'm glad you were able to get here so quickly. Did you get past the reporters without too much trouble?"

"Yes, but they're a persistent bunch, aren't they?"

"They are. But don't you worry about that now. Let me show you to Seth's room."

She came out from behind the counter and began leading us down the hall.

"I'm not sure what you know," she mentioned in a quiet voice, "but he still hasn't opened his eyes. We've been taking good care of him: shaved off his beard, trimmed his hair and bathed him, but you should prepare yourselves for how different he'll look to you. He's quite thin."

"And you still don't know where he was all this time?" Gladys asked. "Or how he ended up on the iceberg?"

Donna shook her head. "I hope we'll be able to get those answers."

Meaning, of course, *I hope he'll live to tell the tale.*

We all followed her down the hall while my stomach rolled with nervous anticipation. Kaleigh took hold of my hand and squeezed it. I wasn't sure if she was seeking assurance from me or attempting to give it. Either way, I was grateful to have her with me.

At last we arrived at room 403, and Donna gestured with a hand. "He's right in there."

I peered around the corner and saw Seth lying on a bed under a blue blanket with an oxygen mask over his face, tubes sticking out of his arms and machines flashing and beeping all around him.

Gladys covered her mouth with a hand and whispered, "Dear God. I can't bear it."

"At least he's alive," I said, rubbing a hand over her shoulder. "And he's with us now."

When she made no move to enter, I slowly stepped forward and approached the bed. Circling around the foot of it, I noticed how thin his body appeared beneath the blanket. Then I came to his side and leaned over to look at his face.

It was indeed unrecognizable.

For a few heart-stopping seconds I stared at him in disbelief, then blinked a few times to try and focus my eyes. My body went strangely numb.

No…something was terribly wrong here. I reached out to lift the oxygen mask away from his face, took a very good look at him, and then set the mask back in place.

On the inside, my stomach was reeling with sickening dread and unthinkable disillusionment, but I did my best to maintain a calm demeanor as I turned to regard Gladys, Kaleigh and Donna.

"This isn't him," I said. "It's not Seth. It's someone else."

Donna's eyebrows flew up in astonishment. "Are you sure?" She rushed in to stand on the other side of the bed and removed the mask again. "Look again. He's very gaunt. It might seem difficult at first, but—"

"No, it's not him. I'm positive."

Gladys approached the bed and stood at the foot of it, staring blankly at me in silence.

"Come closer," I said to her, waving a hand.

Her face was drawn and pale as she took my place and leaned over the man I was certain was not Seth.

"It's not him," she said, agreeing with me. "I would know my son anywhere, and that's not him." In a flash of movement, she whirled around to hug me and sobbed into my shoulder.

"I'm so sorry."

All I could do was hold her close while I kept my eye on Kaleigh, who was slowly moving into the room with an intense look of confusion and curiosity.

"It's not him?" she asked.

"No, honey," I replied.

Donna turned to leave. "I have to let the doctor know. Please stay here. I'll be right back."

Kaleigh wrapped her hands around the shiny chrome bedrail and stared at the man for a long while. She leaned over him and studied the features of his face. Then at last her eyes lifted and she met my gaze.

"If this isn't Dad, who is it?"

"How could you make a mistake like this?" Still sobbing as she spoke, Gladys waved a tissue around in her fist. I rubbed her back, hoping to calm her down. "He was carrying Seth's journal and wallet," I explained to her, "and he had a heavy beard when they found him. It was a reasonable mistake."

"But who *is* this man?" Gladys demanded to know, "and why does he have my son's things?"

"Maybe when he wakes up he can tell us," Kaleigh helpfully suggested.

"That's *if* he wakes up," Gladys replied. "The odds don't look so good right now."

"Shh, Gram," Kaleigh said, holding a finger to her lips. "He's right there. He can hear you."

I regarded my daughter curiously.

"She's right," Donna said. "Let's take this discussion elsewhere."

I couldn't have agreed more.

We followed Donna out and she led us to a lounge area outside the ICU with a television, sofas and some bookcases.

"What if that man doesn't wake up?" Gladys asked. "How will I live with this?" She turned to me. "Surely this is enough evidence to make them send out more search parties. If this man is alive, that means he was in contact with Seth. What if he robbed him, or killed him?"

"He was probably on the plane with him," Kaleigh suggested.

"That makes sense," I said. "There were others as well. Two pilots and a couple of members from the film crew. I can't remember their names, but I'm sure the local authorities can—"

"I can look it up on my phone!" Kaleigh offered, whipping it out of her pocket. "There were tons of news stories about it last year."

"Good thinking," Donna said.

As Kaleigh keyed in the information, I couldn't help but glance back at the room where the mystery man was fighting for his life.

What must he have gone through?

My heart squeezed painfully in my chest.

Please God…He made it this far. Just let him live.

By the time the RCMP officers arrived, we had already determined that the man in room 403 must be Aaron Cameron, a clinical psychologist who was widely known to be George Atherton's personal therapist. The photos of him on the various websites were a dubious match to his current appearance, though we understood that he had changed drastically over the past year due to extreme weight loss and a weathered complexion.

The online articles reported that Dr. Cameron had taken a one-week vacation from his position as a clinical psychologist at a successful medical practice in Boston to be part of the documentary film crew.

Aside from the pilots, the only other passenger onboard, besides Seth, was a producer named Jason Mehta. Based on the photos online, we quickly reasoned that he couldn't be the man who was found on the iceberg because Jason was East Indian with an olive complexion and jet black hair.

Two RCMP officers joined us in the visitor's lounge to interview us about what had occurred.

"What led you to believe that the man who was brought in was Seth Jameson?" the female officer asked Donna.

"That's what they told us on the phone," the nurse replied.

"Who's 'they'?"

"The rescue team that brought him in. They found Seth's wallet and journal in his jacket. He also had a compass and a couple of ice climbing axes."

"Would you be able to identify those as belonging to your husband?" the officer asked me.

"Not likely," I replied. "I hadn't seen him in a while. I don't know what his climbing equipment looked like."

The officer wrote that down, then addressed Donna again. "Do you have those personal items here at the hospital?"

"Yes." She stood up. "I'll go get them."

Gladys raised the tissue to her lips and sat down on the sofa. "Dear God. This is a nightmare."

Kaleigh slid closer and put her arm around her.

I wished in that moment that I had thought to ask to see the wallet and dog-eared picture of me before the RCMP officers arrived, as well as Seth's journal.

God, a journal. What had he written in it?

Donna returned with two climbing axes with yellow handles, and
the compass, wallet and journal in a clear plastic bag. All this, she
handed to the female officer, while the other officer left to verify
Aaron Cameron's identity and seek out and notify his next of kin.

The female officer emptied the bag and set everything on
a table. "Would you mind coming to take a look?" she said to
Gladys and me.

We both approached. I stared down at the brown leather wallet but didn't recognize it—again because I hadn't seen much of
Seth over the past few years. But the compass had been a gift
from me. With trembling hands, I slid it out of the leather case
and turned it over.

So you'll always be able to find your way home...

A lump formed in my throat as I slid it back into the case.
"This definitely belonged to Seth," I said shakily.

The officer flipped through the wallet and removed some
credit cards, receipts, a few dollars and the photograph of me.
When she laid those items on the table, something wrenched
inside of me because the image was worn down to almost nothing.
Perhaps it had gotten wet or had been exposed to the elements.

"That's me," I said, "and that's Seth's driver's license."

"What about this?" she asked, picking up the journal and
handing it to me. "Would either of you recognize his handwriting?"

"Yes, we both would." I took hold of the leather-bound notebook and opened it to the first page, where I saw the words:
Journal of Seth Jameson, along with the date—only a few days
after the crash.

When I turned the next page, however, I was shocked to discover an indecipherable jumble of words. I flipped through the
entire journal and it was like that on every page. It took me a
moment to understand that whatever had been written initially

had been covered up by additional journal entries layered vertically over the horizontal lines.

"It's going to be difficult to read this," I said, "but it looks as if Seth's entries are at the beginning, but later it changes to someone else's handwriting—probably Dr. Cameron's—and he ran out of pages so he started back at the beginning by turning the book sideways."

I handed it to Gladys. "I'm not sure how much of this you want to read—it won't be easy—but I'll bet it contains all the answers we're looking for."

"This is still a missing person's case," the officer interjected, "so we're going to have to keep that as evidence for the time being. It might lead us to your husband."

"Will you send out another search party?" Gladys asked. "Now that we know where Dr. Cameron was found, it couldn't be that far from where the plane went down."

"I'll call it in," the officer replied. "We'll see if we can get some choppers out there today."

"Thank you," Gladys said, breaking down again and turning away.

"In the meantime," the officer added, "let's keep hoping that Dr. Cameron will wake up, because outside of this journal—which looks like it's written in code—he's the only key to finding out what happened to that plane. And we'll handle the reporters. We'll put out a statement that it wasn't your husband who was found."

"Thank you," I replied. Out of the corner of my eye I noticed Kaleigh rise from the sofa and head out of the room. "Where are you going?" I asked.

She stopped and turned. "I'm going to go sit with him because he shouldn't be alone. He needs somebody. Is that okay?"

I glanced at Donna for permission, and she smiled at Kaleigh. "That's a great idea, honey. You go right ahead."

Kaleigh left the lounge while I went to comfort Gladys.

"I don't want to be here," she sobbed into the tissue. "I need to go back to the hotel and lie down for a while."

"I'll take you," I said.

"No," she replied, "you should stay here in case he wakes up. He might be able to tell us something. I'll take a cab, but call me if he comes to."

"All right." I helped her to stand and walked her to the elevator.

⁓⦿⁓

I arrived back in room 403 to find Kaleigh standing over Dr. Cameron's bed. She looked up at me when I entered.

"I've been talking to him," she said, "and asking him to try and come back."

"Come back from where?" I asked.

"From wherever he is right now."

I was careful about how I responded. "Do you think he can hear you?"

"I don't know," Kaleigh replied. "He hasn't moved or anything, but I read a book once about a woman who was in a coma and went to heaven where she saw her dead mom and her dead daughter. She came back after a week because she felt she still had stuff to do here. Her family was at her bedside the whole time and her old boyfriend came and played guitar for her. I wish I had *my* guitar. And I hope Dr. Cameron's family can get here, but for now *someone* should be talking to him, or else he might just think there's nothing to come back to and float away."

I moved to stand beside her and stroked her hair away from her face. "Do you believe in heaven?"

"Yes." She slid me a glance. "Do you?"

"I'm not sure," I replied. "My mom wasn't much of a church goer when I was a kid, but I do pray. I *want* to believe, but I guess I won't really know until I see it for myself."

Kaleigh thought about that for a moment. "But then you won't be able to tell people what you saw, unless you die and come back to life. Maybe Dr. Cameron's there now, and if he wakes up he'll be able to tell us about it. I hope so."

Now I understood why Kaleigh wanted to be here at his side. She'd always had an interest in otherworldly things.

"That would be interesting, if he could tell us," I said. "What was the book called?"

"*The Color of Heaven,*" she replied. "I read it when I spent the weekend with Ellen and Wendy at Aunt Nadia's house last year. She had a bunch of books about heaven and other stuff."

Aunt Nadia wasn't really Kaleigh's aunt—not by blood—but that's what Kaleigh called her because she was like a sister to me and her Aunt Audrey. When my half-brother Alex died, he had donated most of his organs and Nadia had received his heart. There had been a strong bond between Nadia and Audrey from the moment they met because Audrey had been married to Alex.

"Did Gram leave?" Kaleigh asked.

"Yes. She was tired and went back to the hotel."

"But *you* don't want to leave, do you?" Kaleigh asked. "Because I'd like to stay."

I couldn't ignore the note of pleading in her voice, and besides that, I couldn't possibly turn around now and go back to Boston, not when we still knew so little about what happened to Seth and what this man might know of it.

Gladys couldn't let go of the hope that Seth might still be alive and part of me didn't want to give up either, even though my gut was telling me it was a lost cause. Especially now that we had his wallet and journal.

Surely this man must know what happened.

I leaned over the bed and looked carefully at his face.

I should have thought of it when I walked Gladys to the cab, but after about a half hour I realized I hadn't called Josh since we landed.

"Will you be okay here for a little while?" I asked Kaleigh. "I should call Josh and tell him what's happened. I'll have to go outside to use my cell phone."

"I'll be fine," she replied, digging into her bag for her book. "I'm going to read to him now."

"That's a great idea."

I left the room, rode down the elevator and exited the hospital into a private courtyard where there were no reporters. Outside the sun had come out from behind the clouds which lifted the temperature a few degrees above freezing, causing the icicles that hung from the roof to melt and drip on the snow-covered ground.

Choosing a bench in the sunshine, I sat down and dialed Josh's number. He answered right away.

"Hello?" The sound of his voice made me nervous for some reason.

"Hi, it's me. I'm at the hospital."

"I've been waiting for you to call," he said with a sigh of relief. "How's Seth doing?"

I leaned back on the bench. "Well...none of this has turned out exactly the way we were expecting. As soon as we arrived, we came straight to the hospital, but it wasn't even Seth they found on the iceberg. It was someone else. It'll probably be on the news soon."

"You're kidding me," Josh replied. "How could that happen?"

"I'm not sure, because this man hasn't woken up yet, but he had Seth's things. We looked up the crash from a year ago and we're pretty sure he was on the plane. His name is Aaron Cameron and he's a psychologist."

"So he survived the crash…?"

"For a whole year," I replied, "but I'm not hopeful that Seth was that lucky. If he was still alive, why would this man have his wallet and journal?"

"Have you looked at the journal yet?" Josh asked. "Maybe it will tell you something."

"The RCMP took it as evidence," I explained, "but they're also sending out some helicopters to search the area where they found Dr. Cameron. I hope we'll know more soon. In the meantime we're not ready to come home yet. We still need answers."

"Of course," he said. "I understand. Do what you need to do, but keep me posted."

"I will." I glanced back at the hospital doors. "I should go back inside now. Kaleigh's glued to the man's bedside and I want to make sure she's okay."

"What do you mean?"

I let out a sigh. "She's always been fascinated with the afterlife. I think she believes she can help him come back from the light—if you know what I mean. I just don't want her to get her hopes up that there's some kind of miracle happening here. That man has been alone in the wilderness for a year. He might wake up and be a little crazy, or mean and ornery."

"I'm sure she'll be able to handle it," Josh said. "She's a smart kid."

"You're right and I need to give her some credit. She's been very mature about everything so far."

"That's because you're a great mom," he said. "You raised her right."

The tension in my neck and shoulders relaxed slightly. "Thank you. I needed that today."

"It's the truth. Now go and be with your daughter," he said. "And I'm sorry it wasn't Seth. Really I am. Call me when you can."

We ended the call and I looked up at the white puffy clouds drifting across the blue sky, and tried to imagine what it must have been like for that man, floating on an iceberg. How long had he been out there?

He must have spent a lot of time staring at the sky.

⌒

Kaleigh and I remained in the hospital all day, taking turns going to the cafeteria so that one of us was always at Dr. Cameron's bedside.

At nightfall, I looked up from my book when a nurse came in to tell us visiting hours were over.

Kaleigh politely asked if we could stay. "We won't be any trouble," she said. "We'll just sit here with him, that's all. He's been alone for too long. He needs people. He needs a reason to come back."

The nurse's expression warmed and she turned to me. "Your daughter's a very compassionate young lady."

"Yes, she is," I agreed.

The nurse considered Kaleigh's plea. "We're not terribly big on rules here," she said, "especially in a situation like this, but you do need your rest."

"Could we stay until midnight?" I asked, sitting forward in my chair. "Then we'll go back to the hotel, get some sleep and come back in the morning."

The nurse nodded. "That sounds fine, but we'll have to turn down the lights around ten. Let me know if you need anything."

She made a move to leave, but I asked one more question. "What about Dr. Cameron's family? The last I heard, the RCMP officers were trying to locate his next of kin. Have they been contacted yet?"

"I'm not sure," she replied, "but I'll call over to the station and ask."

"That would be great. Thank you," I replied. "Maybe someone's on their way here now."

"Fingers crossed," the nurse replied.

I sat back and continued to read my book.

Around ten o'clock, a different nurse came in to turn down the lights. Kaleigh closed her book and stood up. "It's just as well because I have no voice left. I'm going to go to the lounge for a few minutes and stretch out on the sofa. Can you sit here and take my place?"

"Why don't we head back to the hotel now and get some sleep?" I suggested. "We can come back first thing in the morning."

"No, Mom, you promised we'd stay until midnight," she complained. "I don't want to leave before then."

"All right, all right," I replied, rising from my chair and stretching my arms over my head. "I'll keep an eye on him, but I have to warn you—when the clock strikes twelve, I'm going to turn into a pumpkin."

Kaleigh rolled her eyes at me. "Mom, you seriously just quoted Cinderella to me? I'm *twelve*."

I moved to kiss the top of her head. "And growing up way too fast. I was proud of you today. Have you ever thought of becoming a nurse? You'd be so good at it."

"I don't know, maybe," she replied over her shoulder as she left the room.

I yawned and gazed toward the bed where Dr. Cameron was still lying, comatose.

The heart monitor beeped steadily in the dim light and I listened to the unvarying sound of his breathing from behind the oxygen mask.

Had Kaleigh's constant attention made any difference? I wondered as I approached the bed curiously. She'd been reading to him from a middle grade fantasy novel she'd carried with her on the plane. It probably wasn't a grown man's cup of tea, but perhaps just the sound of her voice was enough to interrupt the constant silence of his coma. I didn't have much scientific knowledge about these things, but I didn't want to rule out the possibility that a human connection might have some value in this situation.

I arrived at the bedside and looked at his face for a long moment, then down at his slender arm where an IV was taped to his hand.

"What happened to you?" I softly asked as I touched his cheek. "I hope you wake up. We're trying to find your family and when we do, I'm sure they'll be very relieved to know you made it home."

I leaned even closer, over the bed, to look at his face again. Gently, I stroked his forehead. "You're safe now. You're in good hands, so it's time to come back. All you have to do is open your eyes."

I waited and waited, but he offered no response.

Not yet ready to give up, I leaned back slightly. "You've been gone a long time. Just think how great a cheeseburger and fries would taste right now. Hot running water? Telephones? Movies?"

Still, he did not wake, so I sat back down in the chair and continued to wait.

It was probably a mistake to close my eyes, but I was so tired after the long flight from Boston and the turmoil of the day, that I simply couldn't stay awake.

Kaleigh must have experienced the same issues because she didn't return from the lounge when it was time to leave at midnight.

It was two o'clock in the morning when I sat up in my chair, startled by the raspy sound of my name spoken from behind the oxygen mask.

"*Carla?*"

I practically leaped out of my chair to lean over the bedrail. "Dr. Cameron?"

He didn't move his head on the pillow, but his gaze shifted to meet mine. He looked like he couldn't quite believe what he was seeing.

I reached out to remove the oxygen mask so he could speak.

"Carla?" he whispered again.

"Yes, I'm Carla," I replied. "You're in a hospital in Newfoundland, Canada. You were found floating on an iceberg a few days ago. We're so glad you're all right. If you'll just excuse me for a minute, I need to go get a nurse."

I probably should have pressed the call button, but I was so frazzled, I set his oxygen mask back in place and ran from the room to the nurses' station.

"He's awake!" I said, skidding to a halt. "Room 403!"

The duty nurse quickly stood but I couldn't wait for her. I pivoted on the shiny white floor and ran back to the room.

"The nurse is coming," I said to Dr. Cameron as I returned to his side.

He blinked up at me and nodded, then lifted his arm off the bed. I immediately clasped his hand.

"You're all right," I said with a smile. "You're home now and you're safe. Everything's going to be fine."

He nodded again, very weakly, and squeezed my hand.

⁓

The medical team asked me to leave the room while the doctor examined Dr. Cameron, so I headed down to the lounge area to wake up Kaleigh.

Shaking her gently, I whispered, "He's awake."

She opened her eyes and blinked up at me. "What time is it?"

"It's just after two in the morning, but I have good news. Dr. Cameron woke up a few minutes ago. They're examining him now."

"Is he okay?" she groggily asked while sitting up on the sofa.

"He seems lucid, if that's what you mean."

"Has he said anything yet? Did you talk to him?"

"He said my name, but other than that he's still pretty weak."

She inclined her head at me. "Did you *tell* him your name?"

In all honesty, it hadn't even registered that my name was the first word he spoken, until she asked me that. A strange shiver ran though me. "No."

"How did he know it was you?" she asked. "From the picture?"

Of course that was it. That's how he knew who I was. He might even have been staring at me for quite some time before I woke up. "I guess."

Kaleigh rubbed her eyes, then stood up. "Can I go see him?"

"Not yet," I replied. "They're still checking him over. Let's just wait here."

She sat back down again. "See? I told you. This is why it's good that we stayed."

I couldn't possibly disagree.

A short while later, the nurse came in to speak to us. "Dr. Cameron's doing well, all things considered. The doctor just finished with him and he's asking for you."

"For *me*?" I asked, pointing a thumb at my chest.

"Yes. You're Carla, right?"

"That's right." Rising to my feet, I asked, "Can I bring my daughter?"

"I don't see why not," the nurse replied. "Just go easy on him. He's sitting up but he doesn't have a lot of strength."

We followed her down the hall and the closer we got, the more hesitant I became. He was a total stranger to us. I'd never met him before and I knew nothing about him, yet my name was the first word he spoke upon waking from a coma. It was a little unnerving.

"Hi there, Dr. Cameron," I said, cautiously entering after knocking on the open door. I noticed they had removed the oxygen mask from his face. "I'm Carla, and this is my daughter Kaleigh."

"I know," he said. "And call me Aaron."

I swallowed uneasily. "Do you remember what happened to you?"

He nodded. "The doctor explained most of it. I just can't believe I'm here. That I actually made it."

I moved to take a seat in the chair by the bed while Kaleigh pulled the other chair closer to sit beside me.

"You must have quite a story to tell," I said. "None of us can figure out how you ended up on an iceberg."

I was struck by the warmth in his eyes as he regarded me in the dim light of the room. "That's kind of a long story."

"Please, if you're too tired..."

"It's all right," he replied, waving a hand dismissively. "They tell me I've been sleeping for days. God knows I should be rested enough. Though I'm still not sure this is really happening. Maybe I'm dreaming. Or I'm dead."

"It's real," I assured him, noticing that Kaleigh had suddenly become shy and quiet. I gestured toward her with a hand. "I'm not sure if you're aware, but Kaleigh was reading to you today. We thought it might help for you to hear someone's voice. I wonder if that helped you wake up."

He met Kaleigh's gaze directly. "Thank you, Kaleigh. That means a lot to me. It's been a long time since I heard the voice of another person. Or read a book for that matter. What was it about?"

She went to fetch it out of her bag, brought it over and showed it to him. "It's called *Princess Callie and the Fantastic Fire-Breathing Dragon*."

"Oh, I love stories about dragons," he replied with interest as he examined the cover. "And this dragon looks pretty friendly."

"He is. His name is Earle and he wears glasses."

Dr. Cameron smiled up at Kaleigh and handed the book back to her.

"We're really glad you're all right," she said as she accepted it.

When she sat back down, I squeezed her hand.

Meanwhile I couldn't help but ponder the fact that this was all very polite and courteous, but what we really needed to know was what happened to Seth. It wasn't an easy question to ask, however.

"So you were on a plane that crashed," I said, hoping to ease into it.

He looked down at his hands and nodded. "You must be wanting to know what happened to your husband." After a pause, he lifted his gaze. "Seth *was* on the plane with me. We sat across from each other. Do you know anything about that yet? I'm not sure what's been discovered since they found me."

I shook my head. "Nothing's been discovered. No one even knows where you landed. There was a search last year but it was called off after about a week when they couldn't find any wreckage. It was all over the news and eventually everyone assumed you went down in the ocean."

"That's not what happened," he said. "We crash landed on an island. It wasn't very big and I still have no idea where it is."

"You say *we*," I replied. "So you weren't the only survivor?"

His gaze shifted back and forth from me to Kaleigh. "No. But there were only two of us that survived the crash——your husband and me. I don't know why I'm surprised you don't know this. I don't know what's what."

Aaron and I stared at each other intensely, and somehow in that moment I knew what he was about to tell me—that Seth had perished sometime afterward.

But I still needed to know how, why and when.

I needed to know everything.

Over the next half hour, Aaron described the horrific events of a year ago when the plane went down. He also explained how Seth had taken charge of the situation and saved them both from a deadly avalanche.

He described the first few days on the island and how they set up camp on top of a small mountain to watch for rescue planes. Eventually they'd returned to the valley in search of food, but had become stranded under a tree in a storm where they were attacked by a lynx.

Lastly he expressed his regret over how everything went wrong the next day, and how Seth fell off the ridge.

"I wish there was something I could have done for him," Aaron said, "but there wasn't. I'm sorry. It was a bad fall."

For a few minutes I wept softly and held Kaleigh, then we wiped our eyes and faced Aaron again.

"What happened to his remains?" I asked. "Did you bury him?"

He hesitated. "I'm not sure if your daughter should hear this."

"Please, Mom," Kaleigh said to me.

I gave Aaron a nod, so after a pause, he continued.

"I couldn't bury him because the ground was frozen. All I could do was cremate him and save his ashes."

I stared at him for a long moment. "That must have been very difficult for you."

He lowered his gaze.

Quietly, I asked, "Were you able to save his ashes?"

I knew it would mean the world to Gladys to finally receive her son's remains.

Aaron's eyes lifted. "I put his ashes in a First Aid kit container, but I lost everything when I hit the iceberg. All my belongings went into the sea except for what I had on me, in my pockets."

"How did you end up on the iceberg?" Kaleigh asked. "Did you have a boat?"

"Sort of," he replied. "After a whole year on the island, I became so desperate to be rescued, I built a raft out of logs and sections of the airplane. I'd seen a few ships go by and I figured I'd take my chances."

"How did you get onto the iceberg?" she asked.

Aaron took a breath and let it out. "I was only out there for a day or two when a family of orcas tried to knock me off my raft—or that's what I thought at the time. I'm not actually sure what they were trying to do. Maybe they were just playing, but they ended up pushing my raft up onto a flat section of the ice. The raft sank after that, so in a way they saved my life."

"You mean killer whales?" Kaleigh asked with fascination.

He nodded. "After I climbed off the raft, I was able to use Seth's axes to get to the top."

"Wow!" Kaleigh exclaimed. "That's *amazing*."

"Is it?" he asked. "I'm still trying to decide if I was extremely lucky over the past year, or extremely *un*lucky."

"I doubt it has anything to do with luck," I mentioned. "You're here today because you were smart and resourceful and did what you had to do to survive."

Maybe he wasn't accustomed to receiving compliments, or maybe he just wasn't used to talking to people, but he didn't respond. All he said was, "Again, I'm very sorry about your husband."

"Thank you." I turned to Kaleigh. "We'll have to tell Gladys all of this in the morning. And no doubt the RCMP will want a report," I said to Aaron. "They may have sent out some helicopters yesterday to search for Seth and the wreckage."

"I'll do my best to tell them where the island is," he replied. "It can't be too far from where they picked me up. What's left of the plane is in a valley, dead center. The pilots' remains will need to be recovered. I'm not sure what happened to the other passenger. His name was Jason and he fell out of the plane as we were crashing. I explored every inch of that island over the past year, but I never found him."

I thought achingly of these people who had died and wondered again how Aaron had managed to stay sane all alone.

"I should warn you," I said, "the media's been all over this story. It's been on all the news channels and online sites."

He seemed surprised to hear that. "Really?"

"Yes, partly because it was George Atherton's plane that went down. You might want to have your incoming phone calls screened."

"Thanks for the heads up."

Kaleigh yawned and laid her head on my shoulder. I stroked her hair away from her face. "I think it's time for us to go back to the hotel," I said. "I'm sure Aaron would like to get some rest."

He watched me in silence as I stood up and gathered our things, and though I knew we had to go, I dreaded walking out the door and leaving him. It pained me deeply to imagine the loneliness he must have endured on the island. I consoled myself with the reminder that there were nurses here and other patients. He was no longer completely alone.

But still, I hated to go.

"Will you come back tomorrow?" he asked.

"Yes," I replied without hesitation. "My mother-in-law might want to meet you as well, if that's all right. She may have some questions about Seth's last days."

"I'd be happy to talk to her," he said.

"And from what I understand," I added, "they're trying to locate your family. I'm sure you'll hear something about that tomorrow as well."

He laid his head on the pillow. "I hope so. After all of this, I'd really like to see my parents. They've probably been very worried."

I felt a heaviness settle in my chest and expand up into my throat. There was so much more I wanted to know about this man and his experiences, but he needed to rest, and so did we.

At least he and his family would be reunited soon. Thank God for that.

"I'm sure they'll want to give you a big hug when they see you," I replied. Glancing discreetly down at his ring finger, I asked, "Are you married? Do you have a wife or children?"

He shook his head. "No, but I hope to remedy that one of these days. If I learned anything on the island, it's that life is short. Chop, chop."

I smiled, approached the bed and clasped his hand. "Well, it looks like you've been given a second chance at everything. I'm happy for you, Aaron. I'm so glad you made it home."

I bent forward to hug him and kissed him on the cheek. My lips lingered there for a moment longer than they should have.

"Please come back tomorrow," he whispered in my ear. The urgency in his voice caused a jolt inside of me.

As I drew away, I felt myself becoming caught in the pale blue of his eyes, and again I dreaded leaving. Something intense and unfamiliar moved through all my nerve endings. I wasn't sure what was causing it, but whatever it was, it felt important. My desire to learn more about this man overwhelmed me.

"I will," I replied. "You have my word."

Fifty

᷍cᴄᷤᷤᷢᷢᷢᷓ᷈

When Kaleigh, Gladys and I arrived at the hospital the following morning, we had to rush past the reporters. We were then met by a grim-faced Donna at the nurse's station on Aaron's floor.

"I'm glad you're here," she said. "We've been waiting for you."

My stomach dropped. "Why? What happened?"

I had visions of Aaron falling back into a coma, or perhaps, because he was so frail, that his heart or some other organ had given out during the night.

The thought of him slipping away now, after coming so far, was like a hard punch to my stomach, and I lost my breath. I felt woozy.

"Come with me." Donna walked out from behind the counter and led the three of us into the lounge. "We've had some bad news." She paused and glanced uneasily at Kaleigh. "Officer Jerome called a little while ago to let us know that they tried to get a hold of Aaron's family. As it turns out, his parents were killed in a collision involving a drunk driver two months ago."

I covered my mouth with a hand. "Oh God, no. Does he know yet?"

Donna shook her head. "Officer Jerome is on her way here to deliver the news, but they were at least able to locate his sister,

Penny. She's making arrangements to fly here, but it might take a while because she lives in Hong Kong."

A lump like a jagged boulder lodged painfully in my throat, and I sank onto the sofa and cupped my forehead in a hand. "That poor man. He's been through so much. What else will he be asked to endure?"

Donna nodded in agreement. "We'll have a grief counselor in the room when we tell him, but I thought it might help for you to be there as well," she said to me.

"Why me?" I asked.

"Because he feels a connection to you."

I felt a connection to him as well. I'd felt it the moment he spoke my name, maybe even before that, but this was not something I wished to say out loud to strangers, or to Kaleigh who might read too much into it. At the moment I was still trying to tell myself that it was the intensity of the situation causing these feelings in me. A sense of empathy about his ordeal.

"We barely know each other," I said, still unable to make sense of it.

Donna absentmindedly fingered the tiny gold amethyst pendant she wore. "You should know that after you left last night, he asked for the picture of you from your husband's wallet. He grew agitated when we told him we didn't have it. The doctor had to give him a sedative to help him sleep."

"But he doesn't even know me," I argued, feeling confused and perhaps even a little alarmed.

Donna sat down next to me and laid a hand on my knee. "I wouldn't worry about this, Carla. He's been through a terrible ordeal and it's not surprising that he would experience some anxiety on his first night. The bright side is that he was quite cognizant of the fact that his anxiety was related to his trauma, and he informed us that he fully expects to suffer from PTSD over the coming months and instructed the nurse to ask the doctor to refer him to a therapist as soon as possible."

"Wow," I said.

"Exactly," she replied. "He's not what I would call irrational. He's very self-aware. But even after all that, he made the nurse promise to get your picture, or a copy of it, back today. He just wants to have it with him, that's all, and he said he knows you're a stranger, but it was either that or another heavy dose of valium again tonight."

I covered my eyes with the palm of my hand. "I can't imagine what this must be like for him. I'm not sure what to do. I wish I could help him, but I'm afraid it's beyond me. I'm just a bank teller."

The lump in my throat mushroomed to the size of a small melon.

"We just need to stay with him," Kaleigh helpfully put in, "at least until his sister gets here. I don't think he should be alone. And the police better bring that picture back or I'll Tweet about how mean they are."

Feeling completely drained, I sat forward and rested my elbows on my knees. "Aside from the angry Twitter threat, Kaleigh, you are an amazingly good person. And you're right. We shouldn't leave him alone. He's been alone for too long."

Gladys wrapped her arm around Kaleigh and gave her a squeeze. "You're a good girl."

"When will the RCMP officer be here?" I asked Donna.

Just then, Officer Jerome walked into the lounge and held up a small plastic bag which contained the barely recognizable photograph of me. "Someone looking for this?"

Wwe decided that I should go to Aaron's room first and
give him the photograph before the others joined
me.

His eyes lit up when I entered. "Good morning," he said, sounding cheerful.

"Good morning to you." I opened the bag, removed the
photograph, and handed it to him. "I have something for
you."

He watched me as I moved around the bed, then he reached
out to take the picture from me.

"Well, *this* is embarrassing," he said. Holding the photo in
his hands for a moment, he stared down at it, then his eyes
lifted sheepishly. "I hope this doesn't make you feel uneasy or
anything. It was the only picture I had of another person the
entire time I was on that island, except for Seth's photo I.D.,
and let's be honest, your face was..." He paused. "Well, you're
much prettier."

The compliment caused a flurry of commotion in me. "You
don't have to explain. I'm glad it helped you."

"It kept me from giving up," he said, "and there were many
times I wanted to."

I wished Officer Jerome could have waited a few more minutes before joining us, but she walked in just then with Nurse Donna and a grief counselor. The three of them surrounded the bed.

—6

Aaron stared blankly at Officer Jerome, and frowned. "That can't be true."

I took hold of his hand and he clasped it tightly.

"I'm so sorry, Dr. Cameron," she replied. "I wish we had better news for you."

He glanced at each of the others in turn, then lastly, his eyes settled on mine.

I shook my head. "I'm so sorry."

He bowed his head and pressed his whole hand over his eyes.

I don't know what came over me, but I couldn't just stand there and hold his other hand. Instead I lowered the rail, slid onto the bed beside him, wrapped him in my arms and pulled him close. He wept quietly for several seconds while I ran my fingers through his hair and stroked his back.

—6

Hours later, I woke from an uncomfortable position on the chair beside the bed and sat forward to check on Aaron.

He was still sleeping, so I relaxed and looked around for Kaleigh. Her backpack was on the floor by the wall, but her chair was vacant. She and Gladys had probably gone to watch television in the lounge.

When I glanced back at the bed, Aaron's eyes were open and he was watching me. "When I was on the island," he softly said, "I used to dream about family dinners and all the things my mother used to cook. She made an amazing potato salad."

"It sounds delicious," I replied.

"Where are your parents?" he asked.

I sat forward. "They're both gone. My father died when I was quite young, though I didn't know him very well. He was never married to my mother because he was married to someone else and had a separate family. My mom died a number of years later, but I do have some family now because I met my half-brother who was part of my father's real family. Alex was a firefighter. Unfortunately he died on the job not long after we met, but I'm still in touch with his parents and his wife."

"So you're no stranger to tragedy either," Aaron said.

"I suppose not," I replied. "I've had to say good-bye to a lot of people, but I guess I've learned to focus on the good things, like my daughter and my job and the friends who love me."

"Seth told me you worked in a bank."

"I do. I'm full-time now and I'm hoping to get promoted to one of the clerk positions. Life is good these days."

Aaron gave a half smile, then closed his eyes and went back to sleep.

I felt a little guilty as I stood outside in the private hospital court-yard, dialing Josh's number.

Why? Because I hadn't been chomping at the bit to call him. To the contrary, I'd been avoiding it since I woke up that morning and I wasn't sure why. I suppose I didn't know how to explain that I wasn't ready to come home yet, even though we'd already received the answers we'd been seeking about what happened to Seth.

"Hello?" he said. "Thank God it's you. I've been waiting all day for you to call. Are you okay? What's going on?"

"I'm fine," I replied. "I'm sorry I haven't been able to call you before now. It's been pretty intense."

"Why? What's happening?"

I switched the phone from one ear to the other and began to wander aimlessly up and down the gravel path.

"They're still waiting for Aaron's sister to arrive from Hong Kong," I explained, "but earlier today the RCMP came to tell him that his parents were killed in a car crash two months ago. Can you believe that? How unlucky can one man get?"

"Wait a second," Josh replied. "So he's awake?"

I pinched the bridge of my nose. Obviously I needed to do a better job at keeping my boyfriend informed.

"Yes, he woke up at 2:00 a.m. last night. And today he found out that his parents died a few months ago."

"Geez, that is rough," Josh replied. "Is he doing okay otherwise? I mean, physically?"

"He's very thin," I told him, "and he took the news pretty hard because it was part of what kept him going all that time— imagining the day he'd be rescued and reunited with his family. Then to finally get here and find out his parents had been killed...? It's hard to comprehend."

I couldn't even continue. The lump in my throat had returned.

"Wow," Josh said. "Have you been able to talk to him?"

"Yes." I paused to collect myself. "He told us everything that happened: that he was on the same flight with Seth, heading to Iceland, and the plane crashed on some uninhabited island in the

Atlantic. Only the two of them survived the crash." I paused. "It's not easy to talk about, Josh. I'm sorry. But Seth fell off a cliff the first week they were there. Aaron had to cremate him. Then he was stranded there. Alone for a whole year."

"*God…*"

I covered my eyes with a hand and shook my head. "I'm sorry, I can't talk about it anymore. I should get back inside."

"Sure," Josh said after a long pause. "Give Kaleigh a hug for me, all right? And call back when you can."

"I will. I'll talk to you later."

I quickly tapped the screen of my cellphone with the tip of my finger and walked back into the hospital.

I was surprised to discover that Nurse Donna had gotten Aaron out of bed while I was gone. He was now up on his feet, doing slow laps around the unit with his IV bag in tow.

"Wow," I said. "You're stronger than you look."

He gave a smirk which I was glad to see, especially today, after he received the terrible news about his parents.

I fell into step beside him. "How are you feeling?"

"Not bad," he replied, "under the circumstances. Maybe tomorrow I can head down to the gym and pump some iron."

It was my turn to chuckle. "Slow down, cowboy. You might want to start slow and work your way up."

"That's probably good advice," he replied, sounding a little short of breath.

"Do you mind taking over for me?" Donna asked me. "Just stay with him in case he tries to overdo it. One more lap should be enough for today. Will you be all right, Dr. Cameron?"

"I'm good," he replied, and I admired his spirit.

Donna left us alone and we strolled past some other rooms. "Some of these people look pretty sick," he said as if he weren't one of them.

I chuckled again. "Not you, though. You're ready to hit the gym."

"That's right," he replied as we continued down the corridor. "But I really hate that you're seeing me like this," he added in a quieter voice.

"Why?"

"Because you're gorgeous and I'm moving around like a ninety-year-old."

I slid him a playful look. "Are you flirting with me, Dr. Cameron?" I asked.

"I'm not sure," he said. "I think I forgot how to flirt. I forgot how to do a lot of things."

"Not everything, surely."

He smiled at me and the lines at the outer corners of his eyes deepened. I felt rather captivated.

"Only time will tell," he said.

We walked a few more steps. "If it's any consolation," I said, "I think you're doing amazingly well and I'm very impressed by your..." I paused, searching for the right word. "Your resilience."

"I appreciate that," he said.

We arrived back at his room and I stood aside to let him enter first.

Glancing briefly up the length of the corridor, I caught a glimpse of Kaleigh peeking her head out the door of the visitor's lounge.

As soon as our eyes met, she quickly darted out of sight. I wondered with some amusement how long she had been watching us.

———⌀———

That night over dinner at the hotel, Gladys asked me when we would be leaving.

"I don't see the point in staying any longer," she said as she raised her beer glass to her lips. "He's told us everything he knows about Seth. There's nothing left for us to do here."

"We can't leave yet," Kaleigh protested. "We have to at least wait until his sister gets here."

"He's not *our* responsibility," Gladys replied. "I'll admit, it's very sad what happened to his parents, but now that he's back in the real world he's going to have to learn to take care of himself, on his own."

"I think he knows better than anyone how to be alone," I reminded her.

"Well, yes," she stammered. "I don't mean to find fault with him. It's a miracle that he survived and I'm happy for him, but I don't see why *we* should have to stay. He's not family to us and I need to get home. I didn't think to ask anyone to water my plants. I should have given a key to my neighbor. And I want Seth's journal," she added. "He was my son. I should have it."

"It was also Aaron's journal," I mentioned, "since he wrote in it just as much, probably more, from what I saw. I think the officers will consider it to be his property."

Gladys rolled her shoulders and went *harrumph*.

Slowly, I reached for my wine glass and took a sip. "But you're right," I said. "There's no reason you need to stay. I can book you on a flight tonight if you want, but I'm not ready to go yet. I agree with Kaleigh. I think it would mean a lot to Aaron if we stayed, at least until his sister arrives which—barring any unforeseen circumstance—should be by the end of tomorrow."

"You mean I'll have to fly back *alone*?" Gladys asked, sounding horrified by the prospect.

"You'll be fine," I assured her. "Just remember to take your shoes off at security, and when you get to Boston, follow the signs that have pictures of suitcases on them, and after that, look for the signs with pictures of taxi cabs."

Gladys picked up her beer and took another swig. "Maybe I'll just stay the extra day and wait for you. As long as his sister arrives tomorrow when she said she would. I don't know why it's taking her so long."

Maybe because Hong Kong is on the other side of the world?

"Whichever you prefer," I casually replied, then I shared a private look with Kaleigh.

—⟨⟩—

I couldn't sleep that night. For hours I tossed and turned on the bed. Unfortunately I couldn't turn on a light to read or watch television because I was sharing a room with Kaleigh and Gladys, and they were both asleep.

As a result, all I could do was stare at the ceiling and mull over the events of the past few days, while imagining Aaron's experiences alone in the wild after Seth fell off the mountain.

I suspected there were many ordeals he hadn't told anyone about—with disturbing details he didn't wish to describe or revisit.

Thoughts of such things ate away at me and when I recalled what he'd said to the nurses about the likelihood that he would suffer from PTSD, I wished there was a way I could drag all the ugly memories up out of his soul, like a fisherman drawing a net out of the water, and take them away, even for one day, just to give him some peace.

Throughout all this late night pondering, there was still another burning question on my mind—a question none of us had dared to ask Aaron. Not even Gladys.

Had Seth uttered any important final words before he died? Did he live long enough to say anything about any of us?

Did he care about Kaleigh and me?

Had he *ever* cared?

CHAPTER

Fifty-three

%

I slipped out of bed at daybreak and went for a run in the early morning chill. It was well below freezing but I had brought my winter running gear and my iPod so I felt comfortable once my blood began to flow.

The music and the oxygen to my brain helped to clear my head, and afterwards I was able to enjoy a hot shower before Gladys or Kaleigh even woke up.

We ate breakfast together, but Gladys decided to stay at the hotel for the day while Kaleigh and I returned to the hospital to visit Aaron. She was emotionally exhausted and I understood her need to have peace and quiet. She said it was like losing Seth twice and I completely understood.

"Has he mentioned anything to you about what happened when he was unconscious?" Kaleigh asked during the cab ride. "Do you think he went to heaven?"

"I don't know," I replied. "He hasn't said anything about it, and I'm not sure he even remembers what happened. He has no memory of being rescued."

"I'm curious," she said, "but I'm afraid to ask him."

"I don't think he'd mind," I replied. "He's used to talking to people about personal things. He's a psychologist, remember?"

She turned her head to look out the window. "I think I might like to be a psychologist someday."

"You'd be good at that," I replied.

"I'd like it better than being a cop," she added. "Not that I don't respect what they do, but it wouldn't be my thing."

I glanced at her with interest. "Whatever you decide to do, just make sure you enjoy it and that you're following your heart."

She turned on the seat to face me. "That's good advice, Mom. You should make sure you're following your heart, too."

Just then, we arrived at the hospital. I stared at her for a few seconds, wondering what she was referring to exactly, then opened my purse to pay the driver while she got out on the other side.

With a little prodding from me, Kaleigh dragged a chair to Aaron's bedside and summoned the courage to ask if he remembered anything from the time he was unconscious.

"No, I'm afraid I don't," he replied, scooping chocolate pudding out of a small bowl on the hospital tray. "When I woke up I was pretty surprised to find myself in this room. At first I thought I was in my cave on the island, then I remembered I was supposed to be on an iceberg. It took me awhile to figure out where I was, and then, when I saw your mom, I thought I *must* be dreaming."

"So you don't remember a bright light?" Kaleigh asked.

Aaron glanced at me. I shrugged, and he returned his attention to Kaleigh. "Are you interested in near-death experiences?" he asked.

She sat forward and nodded. "Yes. Do you know anything about them?"

"Sure," he replied. "I've treated patients who've had them. I would definitely categorize the phenomenon as something we don't fully understand. I do think there's something to it. We just don't know what it is."

"So you believe in the afterlife?"

He set down his empty pudding bowl and reached for his glass of milk. "I really don't know, Kaleigh. There's a lot of research out there on the subject, but it's very controversial. I can recommend a few books for you, if you'd like."

"That would be great. Thank you."

He finished his milk and set the empty glass down on the tray. "As for me, I don't think I flat-lined at any point. No one had to perform CPR on me. I was just very weak and in need of nutrients. So basically, I was just sleeping the whole time."

"I get it," she said. "No white light."

"Nope," he replied. "I don't even remember having any dreams." Then he glanced at me. "Though I might remember something about a cheeseburger with your mom. Was *that* a dream?"

I lifted my eyebrows. "No, it wasn't. I did say something about that, but I didn't think you could hear me."

"I guess I could," he replied, appearing as surprised as I was.

His blue eyes smiled at me and I felt a wash of happiness move through me.

As I looked down at my hands on my lap, I couldn't deny how much I liked this man, yet somehow, it was so much more than that. After everything he'd been through, I was amazed and inspired by his emotional strength and unshakable will to live. What I felt was pure awe, unlike anything I'd ever felt before. It would take me some time to truly understand it.

Later, when Kaleigh went to watch some television in the lounge, Aaron asked if I would take him outside for a walk in the back courtyard. It was frigid out there and the nurses weren't keen on it, but he insisted he could handle it and I didn't doubt him. So they fetched him a pair of OR greens and a jacket.

As we moved together down the hall toward the privacy of the outdoor garden, I was pleased to see how far he had come in just twenty-four hours. They hadn't yet removed the IV tubes from his arm and we still had to drag a bag full of fluid on a rolling stand, but he was eating well on his own and had regained quite a bit of strength.

We rode the elevator down to the ground floor, and I watched his face as we crossed the lobby and approached the glass doors at the back.

"This is strange," he said. "I'm almost afraid to walk out of here. Afraid I'll never be able to get back in."

"You're home now," I assured him, laying a hand on his shoulder.

"Not quite," he replied. "I still have to fly back to Boston. I'm not keen to fly again, as you can imagine. I don't even know if my townhouse is still there. If they thought I was dead, what did they do with all my stuff?"

"I'm sure your sister will be able to answer those questions," I replied.

We arrived at the sliding glass doors and I held his elbow as we crossed the threshold together. As soon as we stood outside in the sun, he stopped briefly to inhale. I saw his breath on the winter air like a graceful puff of smoke.

When he opened his eyes, I again marveled at how clear and blue they were.

"Now *this* feels real," he said. "Now I know I'm not dreaming."

"Of course you're not," I replied, "but you've had an unbelievable experience. Not many people have been through what you have and lived to come home."

His gaze met mine. "I wouldn't wish it on anyone. Although in some ways, I feel transformed."

I nodded and held his arm as we circled the small courtyard.

Aaron and I sat down on a bench that overlooked a dormant winter garden buried beneath the snow. "Can I ask you something?" I said as a seagull soared above our heads.

"Anything," he replied.

"You were the last person to see Seth. What was he like in those final days?"

Aaron gazed up at the sky. "We weren't stranded together very long, so I didn't get a chance to know him that well, but he taught me a lot about wilderness survival. He talked about his climbs up Everest and showed me pictures on his cellphone. He also taught me how to use his compass. A gift from you, I believe."

"That's right," I said, remembering the day I had given it to him.

"I hope you don't mind, but I claimed it after he was gone. I often pulled it out of the casing just to read the inscription on the back. Do you remember what it said?"

"So you'll always find your way home," I replied.

He reached for my hand and nodded. "Yes, and in many ways, those words saved my life. They gave me a sense of direction and hope. The nurse told me it was in one of my pockets when they found me. I should give it back to you, since it belonged to Seth."

"No," I replied without a second thought. "I want you to keep it. *Please.*"

He hesitated, then spoke softly, "Thank you." He gazed into my eyes for a few seconds and I felt as if he were reading my thoughts.

Everything inside me seemed to wobble and come loose.

"You want to know if Seth talked about you," he said.

I felt strangely exhilarated that he had guessed right, but then I thought of Seth and looked down at the cold hard ground.

"Now I feel insecure all of a sudden. I'm afraid you're going to say 'No, he hardly mentioned you at all,' and I'll feel like a fool for asking."

The truth was, I'd felt insecure about Seth's feelings the entire time we were married, and for good reason. Now that I was here with Aaron, however, I wanted to hear the worst. I wanted confirmation about what mattered most to Seth at the end of his life.

What had I been hanging onto all that time, anyway? Was it the simple idea that asking for a divorce would mean accepting my failure as a wife? As a woman who couldn't compete with a mountain?

Or had I tried to protect Kaleigh from feeling that her home was broken? Was that why I hung on?

"You don't need to worry about that," Aaron said. "He talked about you and Kaleigh quite a bit. He had a video of you on his phone that he played for me."

"A video?"

Aaron nodded. "Yes. You were in the Public Garden in Boston near the swan boats, and you seemed happy. You told him you wanted him to buy you a house on a lake with purple flowers."

I swallowed uneasily. "Oh…I'm surprised he kept that video."

I racked my brain to remember how in love we had been in those first few months after we were married. Those were undoubtedly our best days, after he came home from that disastrous climb up K2 and said he wanted to turn over a new leaf. I'd had such high hopes.

I shook my head at myself. "That house on the lake was just a fantasy. I wasted far too much time waiting for him to come home to me when I should have given that up and taken more control of my life."

"*He* never gave up on it," Aaron told me. "He kept re-uploading that video every time he got a new phone."

"Really?" I said. "That surprises me."

"Why?"

"Because he rarely called or wrote those last few years. I didn't think he cared about us at all."

A church bell rang somewhere in the distance and Aaron spoke earnestly. "He did care and he had his own regrets. He told me, just before he died, that he felt guilty about breaking his promises to you, and that he wished he'd been a better father. I believe he wanted to be."

"That may be true," I said, "but wanting to be a better father and actually doing something about it are two very different things." I looked at Aaron. "Do you think he would have come home to us and tried to start over if he had made it home with you? Do you think the experience of crashing in that plane might have changed him?"

Not that I would have wanted that. I don't think anything could have changed my feelings back to what they once were.

Aaron looked away. "I don't know, Carla. But I can at least tell you what his dying wishes were, if you want to know. I think you deserve that much."

I waited with bated breath for him to reveal them to me.

"Just before Seth died, he asked me to cremate his remains and to save his ashes, and when I got rescued, he wanted me to give half of them to his mother, then to find a friend of his named Mike and ask him to release the other half at the top of Everest."

Hearing this from Aaron was like a punch in the gut. Were there no final wishes about Kaleigh and me? I swallowed over my sorrow.

I'd always known the mountain would win.

"I'm not really surprised," I said, looking up. "He was every inch a climber, straight to the bone, and a very good one at that. It was his passion. Though it hurts me in some ways to know what was most important to him, I'm glad he spent his life doing what he loved most. We should all be so lucky."

I looked down at my wedding band, then slid it off my finger, reached for my purse and dropped it into my wallet.

When I set my purse back on the bench, Aaron was watching me intently. I regarded him with a comfortable sigh. "There."

He smiled and squeezed my hand.

"So tell me," I said. "What went through *your* mind when the plane was going down?"

He sat quietly, then scratched his temple with his forefinger. "I remember wishing I'd had children. I even tried to bargain with God and I promised that if I survived, I'd be more open to…" He stopped.

"To what?"

He shrugged. "I don't know. Love, I guess."

"You weren't open to it before?"

"Oh, I was," he replied, "but I went through a rough relationship that ended very badly. After that, I just wanted to focus on work. No more complications or drama."

"Can I ask what happened?"

Squinting in the bright sunshine, he looked away. "She and I lived together when I was in grad school, then she just packed her bag one day, told me she was bored, and left. The last time I ran into her, she was struggling with addiction."

"I'm sorry," I said. "I shouldn't be so nosy."

"It's fine," he replied. "It was a long time ago. Almost eighteen years ago now. I've had a few relationships since then, but nothing ever felt quite right." He grinned at me. "Some analyst, eh? You'd think I'd know what was wrong with me."

I laughed softly. "Maybe it's nothing. Maybe you just haven't met the right person."

He nodded, and we sat in silence for a while, listening to the seagulls overhead.

I was surprised by how tempted I was to lay my head on his shoulder.

A sudden wave of guilt washed over me because I was supposed to be in love with another man—a handsome, heroic police officer who was waiting faithfully for me at home.

My attraction to Aaron Cameron, however…It was distinctly compelling and mystifying, and I believe with all my heart that I might have given myself over to it completely if he had turned to me with those striking blue eyes and kissed me right then.

The hospital doors slid open, and I felt rather shaken as we both looked back.

"It's my sister," Aaron said. He smiled, then his eyes filled with tears.

Mine did as well.

As soon as Penny saw us sitting on the bench, she broke into a run.

I helped Aaron rise to his feet.

CHAPTER

Fifty-five

ᴄᴄ◡ᴄᴄ◡ᴄ

Later that evening, after booking Gladys, Kaleigh and myself on an early morning flight back to Boston, I returned to the hospital to say good-bye.

I don't know why I expected this visit to be straightforward. I suppose I'd been trying to deny how I felt about this man I'd met only a few days ago, because intellectually, I knew it shouldn't be like this. I shouldn't feel so close to him, as if he had been a part of my life forever, or that I was capable of knowing him better than anyone else ever could.

In the courtyard earlier, after a tearful reunion, Aaron's sister Penny had thanked me profusely for staying with him until she arrived. She'd also assured me that she had plans to remain in the U.S. for a number of weeks until her brother was fully recovered, and to help him get his life back in order. She was just so happy he'd survived the ordeal of the past year. And so thankful she'd found him again.

The fact that he had someone here on this planet who loved him deeply filled me with relief, because if she hadn't arrived, I'm not sure I could have left him. I simply couldn't bear the thought of him being alone again after the year he'd just spent on that island. I couldn't breathe when I imagined his loneliness, and I became filled with a yearning that perplexed me.

When I knocked on his door that evening after dinner and announced that I was there to say good-bye, his mouth fell open slightly and the color drained from his face.

Penny left us alone for a few minutes.

Aaron inched himself up higher against the pillows, and I sat down beside him.

The air in the room seemed to thicken as we stared at each other, and I wondered where all the oxygen had gone.

"I can't let you leave without thanking you," he said. "Not just for staying here at the hospital, even after you found out I wasn't your husband. I know it might sound ludicrous, but I don't think I could have survived on that island without you."

My gaze remained fixed on his, but I couldn't find words to speak.

"Am I scaring you?" he asked with a hint of a smile, leaning forward slightly.

"No." I smiled too.

He seemed to relax. "I don't know what I would have done without your picture to look at, the compass to keep me from getting lost, and that video. I must have replayed it twenty times until the battery died. Then, the sound of your voice in my head always calmed me at night. Now I really *do* sound crazy."

"No, it's fine," I said. "I'm glad you're telling me this."

He squeezed my hand. "I wish you didn't have to go."

All at once, I sensed in him a desperation, not unlike what I'd felt in the courtyard earlier when I allowed myself to acknowledge the inexplicable yearning I felt.

I felt it again now.

"Our flight leaves in an hour," I said, running my hands over his, noticing all the calluses.

He nodded, accepting that I had no choice.

We gazed at each other for an intense moment until those blue eyes of his made me feel like I was floating. My body felt weak and shaky.

"Do you mind if I bring Kaleigh in now?" I asked, stumbling over the tangled mess of my emotions. "She's waiting in the lounge and wants to say good-bye to you, too."

"Of course," he replied.

I rose from my chair and quickly left to fetch her.

―⁂―

"I'll miss you," Kaleigh said, bending forward to hug Aaron. "I'm so glad you're okay."

"I'll miss you, too," he replied. "And I won't forget to send you that list of books. I'll need your email address," he said to me.

Kaleigh glanced over her shoulder at me, but I was distracted and flustered. "Of course." I dug into my purse for a pen and paper, wrote it down and handed it to him. "My phone number's there as well."

"I should go," Kaleigh said. "Gram says bye, too." She turned to walk out.

"Tell Gram I'll be right there," I whispered to her, then I moved closer to the bed and held out my arms to embrace Aaron.

It was awkward because I had to lean over the bedrail. Or maybe that's not why it was awkward. Maybe I knew there was something gigantic between us that I wasn't prepared to openly acknowledge.

As I turned to leave, he sat up. "Carla, when I get back to Boston, can I see you? Can we have dinner or something?"

I blinked a few times and my heart began to pound. "I want to," I replied, "but I probably shouldn't. I'm…I'm seeing someone right now."

I simply couldn't lie.

Aaron's lips parted. He stared at me blankly. "I'm an idiot."

"No, you're not," I replied. "I'm sorry, I don't know why I thought you knew that."

Why would he know? I hadn't told him.

He relaxed against the pillows. Although relaxed probably wasn't the right word. It was obvious he was disappointed. Even that word was an understatement.

"So now I know," he said. "Have a good flight, and I'll send that booklist to Kaleigh as soon as I can."

"Thank you, Aaron. Bye." I hesitated, then turned and walked out.

Shortly after takeoff, I gazed out the window at the full moon reflecting off the cold North Atlantic water below.

The starboard wing dipped sharply downward as the pilots steered the plane toward the south.

The glistening dark sea held me mesmerized. All I could think of was Aaron and the terror he must have felt when the plane was going down. I thought of every word we'd spoken to each other over the past two days, and my heart ached as we ascended into the sky and headed for home.

Three Months Later

Kaleigh

Shortly after my thirteenth birthday—while I was enthralled with my weekly group guitar lesson on Friday nights and becoming infatuated with a darkly handsome, seventeen-year-old student with a lip ring—my mom was doing her best to pretend she was in love with a cop who tried way too hard to be perfect husband material.

And perfect father material.

Empirically speaking, I suppose I couldn't deny that Josh was a pretty good catch. He was good-looking by most women's standards, he held down a steady job and wore a uniform. Most importantly, as far as Mom was concerned, he lived here in Boston, had a large, closely knit family, and held no secret ambitions to run off to the Himalayas and scale mountains.

Mom liked that he was so committed and reliable, and it didn't hurt that her friends and co-workers were all thrilled for her, including Aunt Audrey and Nadia, who loved the idea of welcoming a cop into the family.

"He has so many great stories to tell at dinner parties," I heard Audrey say one night when I went to the kitchen to make popcorn for me and Wendy while they were drinking wine in the living room. Audrey gushed over how great Josh looked in his gun belt, and how wonderful it was that Mom had finally turned a corner and let go of my dad.

Meanwhile, I was the only one who knew the real truth—that Mom had been deeply affected by our brief encounter with Dr. Cameron in the hospital a few months earlier, and she hadn't forgotten him. Not by a long shot.

I'd been affected by it myself, and I still wasn't sure why that experience seemed so colorful in my otherwise lackluster life.

I couldn't stop wondering if it had been our voices that brought Aaron back from the abyss. Or my mom's touch? And why did all of this happen? Were the three of us meant to cross paths? Had it been fate?

I didn't mention anything like that to Mom because I knew what she'd say: that I didn't know what I was talking about because I was a thirteen-year-old girl with an overactive imagination who had been reading too many books about mystical things.

But I'd seen them together with my own two eyes, and I knew my mother better than anyone.

Something in her had changed after we flew home. She'd grown quiet and adopted a habit of staring off into space. Sometimes I would catch her in the kitchen, leaning against the counter while a pot of something boiled over on the stove, right beside her. She wouldn't even notice. She was a million miles away.

I often asked her what she had been thinking about. A few times she admitted openly that it was Aaron. She said she was imagining his flight from the polar bear, or his climb up the iceberg with the killer whales circling below.

Though we didn't hear from Aaron at all, except for the list of books he sent via email, we did hear from Gladys about the journal.

Two months after we arrived home, she called Mom and said that although Aaron had stubbornly refused to hand over the journal to anyone, he had been kind enough to transcribe the early entries Seth had written on the island. Aaron had mailed the pages to her, which she photocopied and shared with Mom, who shared them with me.

The last entry was written under the tree when they were lost and trapped in a storm. My father's final words were: *I said another prayer.*

He died the next day, and I'm pretty sure God must have been listening because that was around the time I had the dream about my dad. He'd seemed at peace about saying good-bye. He'd almost seemed happy. I suspected he was climbing a mountain somewhere in the high altitudes of heaven.

We didn't talk about the journal again.

"Why don't you send Aaron an email just to say hi?" I suggested one evening over dinner.

It was *me* who brought Aaron up that night. Probably because Mom was talking about Josh too much lately and had asked if I wanted to spend Saturday night with Ellen at Nadia's house. I suspected Josh had something romantic planned.

Mom shook her head at me. "I don't think that would be appropriate."

I poked at my carrots with my fork. "Why not? Unless you're referring to the fact that he asked you out on a date before we left, and you said no because you were seeing someone else."

She picked up her water glass and narrowed her eyes at me. "How would you know that?"

I inclined my head. "Seriously, Mom? You must have known I would eavesdrop outside the door."

She chuckled softly and focused her attention on cutting her pork chop. "Well...I *am* seeing someone else."

"Which is why you don't want to lead Aaron on," I finished for her, even though it drove me nuts that she might be missing out on something that could be her destiny.

Okay, okay...

Maybe I *was* overly romantic and thought I knew everything about love because I'd found my perfect soul mate—the mysterious and aloof guitar player named Malcolm from my Friday night practice sessions. Unfortunately he didn't seem to know I existed, but I had a plan for that.

I had a plan for Mom, too. I wanted her to be with Aaron, not Josh, so I wasn't going to stop mentioning him. Not if he was destined to be the great love of her life, maybe even a match made in heaven.

Most of me knew how silly that sounded, but I'd been thinking about Aaron a lot lately, maybe because I was starting to worry that Mom was forgetting him. It had been almost three months since we'd seen him.

I didn't *want* her to forget him. And I don't think she did either.

Twelve Days Later

❧

Carla

Sometimes I wonder if things are meant to happen a certain way, or if there is something in us—maybe some sort of psychic ability—that leads us to do a certain thing, even if we don't understand why we're doing it at the time.

I've often asked myself that question regarding the day I left work early because of a sinus infection that had come on rather suddenly.

I'll be the first to admit that it wasn't very serious and I probably could have suffered through the last two hours at my desk. But I didn't tell my boss that. I exaggerated my symptoms, just a tad, and threw in a migraine headache to go along with it.

I wasn't making it up, not entirely. The stuffy nose really was uncomfortable, but later I wondered if there was more to it than that. If somehow fate was poking at me. *Hey you. You should go home.*

I'd been having a hard time concentrating anyway. Earlier that day, Josh had texted and asked if I could have dinner with him that night. He wanted to take me to one of the most expensive restaurants in the city.

When I asked what the occasion was, he texted me back and sent this reply: I want to ask you something.

From that moment on I was pretty useless at work because I couldn't stop thinking about what he might want to talk about.

"You think he's going to propose, don't you," Audrey said when I called her during my lunch hour. "If he does, will you be ready for that?"

"I don't know," I replied, sitting down on a bench in the mall with a bag full of shampoo and toothpaste I'd just bought. "We've only been seeing each other for six months, but he's an amazing guy. I'd be crazy to say no."

"Yes, he is an amazing guy," she replied. "But I know you, Carla. You're not sure. I hear it in your voice."

I switched the phone from one ear to the other. "I can't help it. It's a big step and I don't want to rush into anything. And there's Kaleigh to consider. I don't want to force a new dad on her and I know she's not crazy about Josh. She just tolerates him."

"She's only thirteen and girls that age are known to be prickly."

I glanced up at the crowds walking past, everyone hurrying back to work.

"Let me ask you something," I said into the phone as I rose to my feet. "Did you have any doubts about marrying David?"

Audrey answered the question without missing a beat. "It was my second marriage," she said, "and sure, it's not easy to let go of all the baggage that comes with having been married before, no matter how the first one ends. But when David opened that ring box and got down on one knee, there was absolutely no doubt in my mind that I wanted to be his wife and be with him forever. He barely had a chance to finish proposing before I said yes."

I slowly headed back toward the bank. "I was kind of hoping you'd tell me you had doubts."

"Sorry," she replied. "But if that's how you're feeling, maybe you need to tell him that."

I paused. "I don't want to lose him. He's a good guy."

"*A good guy?*" she responded. "There are plenty of good guys out there, but that's not why you marry someone. You marry him because you love him and he's your soul mate and you can't imagine your life without him."

I thought about that for a moment. "I can't really imagine my life without Josh in it."

"Is that because you love him, or because you don't want to be single? There's a difference."

I rounded the corner in the mall and entered the bank. "I think I'm coming down with something," I replied, and sneezed.

"Bless you," Audrey said. "And maybe that's exactly what you need—a cold to buy yourself time to think about this. You could always tell Josh you're sick and suggest he wait until the weekend."

"Would that make me a coward?" I asked as I headed down to the staffroom.

"No, it just makes you cautious, and there's nothing wrong with that. But let me ask you something else," she said.

"Sure."

There was a pause on the other end of the line. "Are you still thinking about Iceberg Man?"

I reached the bottom of the steps and smiled distractedly at one of my co-workers. "All the time."

"Then you should give him a call," Audrey said. "Go and visit him. Now that he's back in the real world, see if there's something there, because you can't marry another man until you know for sure he's the one. Or not the one."

I opened my locker and placed the shopping bag inside. "Thanks, Audrey," I replied.

What a relief it was to hear someone else make the suggestion, because I was beginning to think I was losing it, feeling strangely interested in a man I'd known for only two days, and in very strange circumstances. I couldn't explain it, but there was no getting him out of my head.

An hour later, after cancelling my dinner with Josh, I was on my way home from work early with a totally legitimate sinus infection.

I had to be careful driving through intersections, because I kept replaying in my mind all the conversations we'd had, and I didn't want to barrel through another red light.

I even started to fantasize about conversations I *wished* we'd had. All the things I wanted to talk to him about. I just wanted to hear the sound of his voice—that riveting, velvety voice.

As I dug my key out of my purse and walked into the apartment, I felt a great weight lift from my shoulders, and a thrilling ripple of anticipation moved up my spine at the thought of calling Aaron.

I wondered what he looked like now after three months. He'd probably gained some weight.

My excitement was curtailed suddenly, however, when I heard panicked whispers coming from Kaleigh's room. Sensing immediately that something wasn't right, I went straight to her door and opened it.

Imagine my shock to find a boy in her bedroom—a boy I'd never seen before.

But wait…This was no *boy*. He had to be at least seventeen, and there he stood in all his glory with a black leather jacket and faded jeans, eye makeup and body piercings.

Kaleigh hastily leaped off her bed. She wore skinny jeans, my brown leather boots with heels, and a long cashmere sweater that was also mine.

And makeup.

"Mom. What are you doing here?" she asked in a panic. "You're supposed to be at work." She turned white as a sheet.

"Who's this?" I asked with a sick feeling in the pit of my stomach.

"This is Malcolm," Kaleigh replied, gesturing toward him with a hand. "Malcolm Watson. We met in guitar class."

I looked him over from head to toe. My eyes settled for a moment on his heavy black combat boots, which he'd not bothered to remove when he came in.

Under normal circumstances I would smile and welcome a friend Kaleigh brought over, but this was not one of those times. What I really wanted to do was tell this kid to get the hell out of my apartment. *Right now. This second. Before I wrung his neck.*

I glared at him intensely. "How old are you?"

"Seventeen," he replied in a low, husky drawl.

I folded my arms across my chest. "Do you understand that my daughter is only thirteen? There are laws you know."

"*Mom!*" Kaleigh shouted.

Her charming gentleman caller frowned at me. "*What?*"

My blood pressure was about to hit the roof, and I could feel a hot blaze searing my cheeks. "She's thirteen! And by the look of you, I think this would qualify as statutory rape."

He blinked a few times in shock, then spoke defensively. "We didn't do anything. Honest. We were just talking."

"Oh sure," I replied. "Tell that to the judge."

"Mom!" Kaleigh screamed again, "Stop! We weren't doing anything! He's just a friend!"

Then the boy—Malcolm was it?—turned to Kaleigh. "You told me you were sixteen."

Oh, God. I cupped my forehead in a hand and closed my eyes.

To my surprise, Kaleigh didn't try to explain anything to me. She was more concerned about what Malcolm thought as he stormed past me to leave.

She followed him out. "I'm sorry, Malcolm!" she cried. "I didn't mean to. I just wanted to spend time with you, that's all."

"You lied," he said flatly without turning around as he reached the door and pulled it open.

"Please don't go!" she said. "Can't we talk about it?"

He left the apartment without responding, but she followed him to the elevator.

"Kaleigh!" I shouted, grabbing hold of her sleeve to try and stop her.

"Wait!" she cried to him.

I'd never heard her sound so desperate before.

I hurried into the hall. Malcolm was pressing the elevator button over and over while Kaleigh cried and begged him not to leave.

Ping! The elevator doors slid open and he couldn't step on fast enough. Kaleigh remained in the carpeted corridor crying her eyes out. "Please Malcolm, I'm sorry! I was going to tell you! I wanted to!"

The doors closed and she buried her face in her hands and wept.

I was in complete shock by this point and had no idea how to handle this. Part of me wanted to march down the hall, drag my daughter by the ear, send her to room and ground her for life.

Another part of me wanted to comfort her and tell her everything was going to be okay. He wasn't worth it. There would be other boys.

But I knew nothing about this kid.

Who the hell was he, and how long had this been going on?

ᴄ⌒ᴐ

Kaleigh's last words to me that night were, "You don't understand *anything*!"

This was followed by the slamming of her door in my face,
and my own internal struggle between red-hot fury and compassion,
because I remembered what it felt like to be thirteen. Everything
seemed so monumental, so catastrophic when things didn't go the
way you wanted them to. It felt like the entire future of the universe
hinged on one moment when nothing else mattered or existed.

The first thing I did was call Audrey. "I don't know what to
do," I said. "She's so angry and upset, but she broke every rule in
the book inviting that boy up here when I wasn't home."

"Do you think anything happened?" Audrey asked.

"I'm not sure. No. At least it didn't look that way when I
walked in. They were frazzled, but they had their clothes on. She
said they were just talking."

"Well, that's good at least. What do you know about him?"

"Nothing, except that he takes guitar lessons and bears a
frightening resemblance to Sid Vicious."

"Wonderful," she replied. "Have you called Josh yet? Maybe
he can look him up and tell you if he has a record or anything."

"I haven't called him yet, but surely he wouldn't be able to tell
me anything. The kid's a minor."

"You should call him anyway. Are you going to be okay?"

"I don't know. I'm not sure if I can handle the teen years by myself. I'm feeling a bit intimidated."

"You know you can always count on David and me for anything," Audrey said. "Just say the word and we'll be there."

"Thanks. I think I'll call Josh now. I'll let you know if there's anything to report."

I called in sick the next morning and got Kaleigh off to school without too much drama, though she barely said more than two words to me. She ate her cereal in silence, and I worried that she might walk out the door and never come back.

Maybe she'd skip school and run off to live on the streets with Malcolm What's-His-Name. I could just hear her now as she ran to meet him under a bridge somewhere. "All we need is love."

Maybe I'd become a cynic, but I truly believed that love wasn't nearly enough.

Josh knocked on my door around 10:00 when I was sitting on the sofa in my bathrobe, drinking my second cup of herbal tea.

I rose to greet him and apologized for my appearance.

"Don't be silly," he said, setting a plastic bag on the kitchen counter and pulling me into his arms. I noticed he held a manila envelope in his hand. "You know I don't care about that. How are you feeling?"

"I've felt better," I replied. "The stuffy nose is nothing compared to what's going on in here." I laid a hand over my heart.

"Don't worry," he said. "I'm here to take care of you. I looked up the kid and I have some news. I also brought you some popsicles and chicken soup."

I felt my shoulders relax. "Thank you."

"No problem. Now let's go sit down and have a talk."

We moved into the living room but I had to sweep a pile of dirty tissues off the coffee table into a waste basket before I sat down. "I don't want to breathe on you," I said.

"I have a killer immune system," he replied. Then he sat down and rested his elbows on his knees, stared at me for a long moment.

"What did you find out?" I asked.

He pulled some papers out of the envelope. "This is confidential, and I'm trusting you to keep this to yourself, but you need to know. I have a picture here. Is this the guy?"

I looked at it and nodded.

"I figured this was him. It's not great news, but it's not terrible either. He doesn't have a record. He's never been arrested for anything, but he's had a hard life. His mother's an addict and Malcolm's been in and out of foster homes since he was three years old."

"That's horrible," I replied, reaching for the picture of Malcolm which looked like it had come out of a middle school yearbook.

"But he's seventeen," Josh said, "and he has no business being around Kaleigh."

"She told him she was sixteen," I explained, setting the picture down on the coffee table. "He seemed pretty angry about that when he found out, so I can't exactly put all the blame on him."

"Still..." Josh said, sliding the documents back into the envelope. "He's not someone you want her spending time with. He lives in a rough neighborhood and his new stepdad was charged for domestic assault against his previous wife. It's not a good situation."

I exhaled heavily and slouched back on the sofa. "I can't believe any of this is happening. Six months ago she was still my little girl, wanting to be tucked in."

He reached forward and touched my knee. "Let's just hope this is the end of it. Maybe you scared him off."

"I hope so," I replied. "Though I do feel sorry for him. I feel badly about how I spoke to him when it's obvious, he didn't know how young she was."

"You did what you had to do," Josh said. "Now you have to deal with Kaleigh. You might want to think about setting some tighter boundaries and stricter rules and consequences. She's at a vulnerable age. Any chance you can move her out of that music school?"

I pinched the bridge of my nose. "She loves her teacher."

"Just think about it," Josh said, then he rose to his feet. "I'm sorry but I have to get going. Are we still on for dinner Saturday night?"

I stood up as well and said, "I think so," as I escorted him to the door.

He stopped and turned. "You *think* so? Don't jump up and down with excitement or anything."

I reached into my pocket for a tissue and wiped my nose. "I'm sorry, Josh. I'm just not feeling the best."

He stared at me for a moment. "Is there something wrong? You've seemed distracted lately."

"Have I?"

I felt as if he was scrutinizing my expression and was contemplating the logistics of dragging me downtown for a lie detector test.

"Yeah," he said. "Ever since you came back from Canada. You're different."

Again, he focused steadily on my eyes, and I had to look away. "Everything's fine," I told him. "It's just been a difficult time. First we thought Seth was dead; then he wasn't; then he was..."

There was much more to it than that, of course, but I didn't want to say anything because I still didn't have my feelings sorted out.

Josh nodded, but I suspected he didn't really believe me.

He kissed me on the cheek and pointed at the bag he'd set on the kitchen counter. "Have some soup. I'll call you later."

As soon as I shut the door and locked it behind him, my cell phone beeped to let me know a text had come in. I moved to the coffee table and picked it up. It was from Kaleigh.

Mom, he was nice. I'm really sad.

My heart split in two, straight down the middle.

I know, honey. We'll talk when you get home.

"I knew it was wrong," Kaleigh told me, lying on her side in bed, curled up in a ball and squeezing her pillow under her cheek, "but I knew he wouldn't see me if he knew how old I was. Now he won't even answer my texts."

I was at least impressed that the kid had the good sense not to.

"I know it's hard," I said, "but it's better that he found out now, before things went too far."

"What do you mean by things?" she angrily asked. "You mean before we had *sex*?"

I took in a deep breath and let it out. "Yes, I suppose that's what I mean."

"We weren't doing *that*," she insisted. "All we ever did was walk around the neighborhood and talk about all kinds of cool things like books and movies. I told him about the books I read that Aaron recommended—you know, about near-death experiences. A few days ago we played guitar in the park after school. Mom, really, he was the nicest person I ever met, and he's had a rough life. He doesn't have a dad either. Except now he has a step-dad who gets drunk all the time, and Malcolm hates that kind of stuff. He's really smart."

"But you don't know him very well," I said.

"Yes, I do!" she cried, sitting up and wiping a tear from her cheek with the back of her hand. "*You're* the one who doesn't know him. You think he's a pot head or something, just because of the way he dresses."

"I don't think that."

"Yes, you do. I saw the way you looked at him, but he's *not* a pot head. He's a great guitar player."

"And he lives in a rough neighborhood," I said.

"I know that, but how do *you* know that, and what does that have to do with anything? Did Josh look him up? Even if he did, I don't care what he told you—but how can you be so heartless?"

"I'm not heartless," I replied. "I do feel badly for him. Honest. But that doesn't mean it's okay for you to see him the way you want to see him. You're too young."

"I'm not too young," she argued. "I'll be fourteen in ten months."

"And he'll be eighteen by then. You should be with boys your own age, honey."

She shook her head at me and lay down again. "You don't get it. You don't understand anything."

"I do understand," I replied, "and when I was your age I fought with my mom, too, every time she wouldn't let me do what I wanted to do. It comes with the territory, Kaleigh, but please have some perspective. You won't be thirteen forever, and with every year, I'll relax the rules and eventually you'll have all kinds of freedoms you don't have now. And it's not that far off. Just be patient and let me be a good mom, okay?"

She let out a huff and turned over the other way with her back to me. "I want to be alone," she said. "No offense."

For a moment I sat on the edge of her bed wondering what I could possibly say to ease the rift between us, but I knew there wasn't anything that could fix it. At least not today. This would take time, and I hoped she'd get over Malcolm Watson sooner rather than later.

Friday morning, while I was in the bathroom putting on my makeup for work, Kaleigh burst through the door with her cell phone.

"He texted me!" she exclaimed in disbelief.

"Who did?" I asked with dread as I lowered my mascara and turned to face her.

"Malcolm. He finally replied. He said he'd be willing to talk to me after practice tonight, but only if you say it's okay. He said we could meet at the Starbucks across the street from the music school. Can I go, Mom? Please? I just want to tell him I'm sorry. I want us to be friends, that's all. I told him that, and that's why he said yes. You can even park outside and watch us from the car if you want. Just don't say no."

Oh, Lord. Maybe I should have been a tougher parent for the past thirteen years. Josh had recommended that I increase the rules and set tighter boundaries, but all my instincts as a mother were telling me to give her this space. To trust her to handle this in a mature and responsible manner.

Maybe that wasn't possible for a hormonal thirteen-year-old, and maybe I would live to regret my decision, but in the end I said yes—with every intention of sitting in my car and staking out the coffee shop.

Kaleigh

It was hard to concentrate on school that day. All I could think of was Malcolm, and my heart nearly beat out of my chest later when he walked into the music room in his black leather jacket with his guitar case slung over his shoulder.

He saw me from across the room and nodded, then took a seat next to someone else on the other side of the circle.

Afterward, as we were packing up, I approached him.

He barely looked at me. "I'll meet you over there."

Feeling disappointed, not even sure if he would actually show up, I walked over by myself and ordered a hot chocolate.

When he arrived ten minutes later, I breathed a sigh of relief.

"Hey," he said as he sat down across from me with a coffee. "Do you know your mom's sitting out there watching us?"

"I know," I replied. "It was the only way she'd let me come."

He tapped his finger on the cardboard sleeve and glanced around impatiently. "What do you want, Kaleigh?"

"Just to tell you I'm sorry."

"You shouldn't have lied to me in the first place," he said.

"I know, but you never even looked at me or spoke to me until I pretended I was older—it was like I was invisible in class every week—and then I *wanted* to tell you the truth, but I was afraid you'd be mad."

He shifted uncomfortably on the seat. "We can't be friends, you know."

"Why not? I said I was sorry. Can't you forgive me?"

"It's not that," he replied. "Even if I do forgive you, it would be weird. I'm not hanging around with a thirteen-year-old."

I looked down at my hot chocolate. "But I like talking to you."

I glanced up and caught him staring at me, but he quickly looked away. "I liked talking to you too, but this is stupid. You shouldn't be texting me."

"Malcolm—"

"Was everything else a lie?" he asked. "Did you lie about the books you read, or that lady you know who had a heart transplant and dreamed about her donor, or your father being dead?"

The fact that we both had dead fathers was what had struck a bond between us the first day we talked after class, and I hated that he thought it wasn't true.

"No," I replied. "I didn't lie about any of those things."

We sat for a little while, saying nothing. He removed the plastic lid on his cup to let it cool.

"How *did* your father die?" I asked. "You never said."

He shrugged. "I don't know. When I was young, my mom used to tell me he died in a car accident, but his name isn't on my birth certificate, so I'm not even sure he is dead. He's probably some loser she didn't want me to meet, or she doesn't even *know* who it is. Last year, she told me he died in a plane crash, but she always says stupid stuff when she's drunk. She's a compulsive liar."

"Really?" I said with a strange little lurch in my belly. "What plane crash?"

"I don't know. It was on the news. They never found out what happened to the plane, which is why I think she said that. I don't believe her, though. I never believe anything she says."

In that moment, I couldn't take my eyes off him. I was mesmerized by the familiar way he held his coffee cup, the way he spoke, and the way his blue eyes seemed to reveal so much about what he was thinking and feeling.

"I should go," I said, reaching for my guitar case and glancing out the window at my mom who was still sitting outside in her car waiting for me. "But are we okay?" I asked as I stood up. "Can we be friends now?"

He considered it a moment. "Sure, I guess. But I don't want to hang out or anything."

"That's okay," I replied. "I'll see you in class next week?"

He stood up as well. "Yeah, whatever."

I let him leave first, then I walked out of the coffee shop to go talk to Mom.

"Do you think it's possible?" I asked as we pulled away from the curb. "Did Aaron ever tell you if he had a kid?"

Mom was disconcertingly quiet, then she shook her head. "He never mentioned that, but he did tell me about a woman he was involved with a number of years ago who left him, and she later had substance abuse problems."

"Are you serious?" I said, turning in my seat to face her. "How long ago was that?"

"He said about eighteen years."

"Then this makes total sense! Malcolm could be Aaron's kid, and he doesn't even know it."

"Hold your horses," Mom replied, waving a hand to settle me down. "We have no idea if that's true or not, and we can't go poking into other people's lives."

"But what if it *is* true? Poor Malcolm never had a dad and he had a horrible childhood. He hates his stepdad and his mom is drunk all the time. If you were Aaron, wouldn't you want to know?"

Mom thought about it as she flicked the blinker and turned left into our neighborhood. "Yes, I definitely would."

As soon as we walked through our apartment door, after a tense ride up the elevator, Mom went into the kitchen and filled the kettle at the sink. "I don't know what to do," she said when I locked the door behind us.

I set down my guitar case and followed her into the kitchen where she was reaching for a mug and a box of tea in the cupboard. I moved to the fridge to get some orange juice.

Mom leaned against the counter and chewed on her thumbnail, thinking intently while she waited for the kettle to boil.

Then she looked up. "Could you text Malcolm and ask him to ask his mother about it again? Don't tell him why. Or maybe just tell him that you knew someone from that crash and you're curious about it."

"I'll have to tell him the truth," I said, "that it was my dad on the plane." Suddenly I felt my forehead furrow with concern. "Wait a second, you don't think Dad could be…?"

"No, not a chance," Mom said. "Eighteen years ago, your father was still living in Australia. He didn't move here until the year before you were born."

I nodded with relief and pulled out my phone.

Fifteen minutes later, my phone beeped.

I picked it up and saw that it was a text from Malcolm. Swinging around to turn my back on Mom, I tapped the icon and read his message.

I asked her and she said it was a guy she lived with once. But it doesn't matter because he's dead anyway.

I turned and showed the message to Mom.

"They don't know he was rescued," Mom said. "Don't his parents watch the news?"

"He says they drink all the time."

Mom gave me a look of impatience that was directed at them, not me. Then she began to pace around the kitchen. "Can you text him back and get him to ask her what the man's name was?"

I quickly keyed in the question.

A few seconds later I received a reply. I can't because my step-dad just went ballistic and kicked me out.

I showed the message to mom.

"Oh, Dear Lord," she said. "Text him back and ask if he's okay."

A few seconds later another reply came in. I held the phone up.

I'm fine. I'm at the park. Just walking around.

I held the phone up. Mom read the text and immediately scooped her keys up off the counter.

"Grab your jacket," she said. "We're going to pick him up right now."

Sixty-three

Carla

My heart pounded like a hammer when I sat down at the computer to send an email to Aaron. We hadn't spoken in a few months, not since the day we said good-bye at the hospital in Newfoundland. Other than that, our only exchange had been through email when he sent the promised list of books to Kaleigh.

She'd borrowed them from the library, blew through them in a couple of weeks, and sent him a personal thank you note, also via email. That was the end of our correspondence, though he was never far from my thoughts.

And now, here I sat, possibly with his biological son sleeping on my sofa, my fingers poised on the computer keyboard, feeling both excited and terrified about communicating with him again.

Carefully I composed a message, then went ahead and pressed send, and stared intently at the computer screen.

Five minutes later, a reply came in.

Hi Carla. So nice to hear from you. Yes, I am well, thanks for asking, and I'd love to talk with you. Is now too late? I'm still awake if you want to chat. Here's my number: 555——

Without hesitation, I reached for the phone and dialed.

L ike a sling shot, my telephone conversation with Aaron sent me straight back to exactly how I'd felt during those intense hours we spent together in the northern hospital.

He was surprised and pleased to hear from me, of course, and I allowed us a few moments to catch up before I brought up the subject of Malcolm.

I told him about Kaleigh doing well in school and thanked him for transcribing Seth's journal entries for Gladys. We all appreciated it very much, I told him. Then I apologized for not keeping in touch.

"No need to apologize," Aaron said. "I understand." We left it at that.

Aaron then told me he'd used a generous private settlement he'd received from George Atherton to buy a house in Claremont, New Hampshire—a small town with a population of about 13,000, where he'd already joined a small medical practice and was working part-time.

"I decided I didn't want to live in the city anymore," he explained. "It was too noisy. I thought maybe I'd wallow in it after the silence on the island, but that's not how it turned out. I do like going to the supermarket, though," he added with a smile in his voice. "That, I definitely wallow in."

"I'm glad to hear all that," I replied, finding myself wallowing in the simple cadence of his voice. Before I knew it, a half hour had passed and I still hadn't mentioned the seventeen-year-old who was sleeping on my sofa.

I wasn't sure how to introduce the subject, so I decided to begin with this: "You must be wondering why I'm calling."

Aaron was quiet for few seconds. "I am a little curious, yes."

I inhaled deeply and gazed up at the ceiling. "This is going to seem like a strange question, but do you know a woman named Meg Watson? She lives here in Boston."

Again, Aaron was quiet. "Yeah. She's the woman I told you about. The one I lived with after college. I haven't seen her in years, though. Why?"

"When, exactly, did you live with her?" I asked. "I know you told me, but I just want to check again. How long ago was it?"

He paused to think about it. "Eighteen, nineteen years ago. Why, Carla? What's this about? Is she okay?"

I sat up and slowly answered, "Yes, she's fine, but…" I paused. "Aaron, she has a son."

My heart thumped against my ribcage.

"I knew she had a child…" he replied, trailing off. "But what are you saying?"

I sat back in my chair and gazed up at the ceiling. "Maybe I should just tell you about him. His name is Malcolm and he's seventeen years old. Kaleigh met him at guitar class." I hesitated briefly before continuing. "I'm not sure how to tell you this, Aaron—it seems I'm always delivering difficult news to you—but I think there's a chance you might be Malcolm's father."

After about twenty minutes of disbelief, anger, sorrow and happiness—and a continuous discussion about what this could mean for Aaron and Malcolm's future—I insisted on driving Malcolm up to Claremont the following morning.

"He's sleeping on my couch right now," I said, "and he'd like to meet you."

"I'd like to meet him, too," Aaron replied, his voice choked with emotion.

Though Aaron had given us excellent directions on how to find his house and I had GPS in the car, it still took help from Kaleigh as my front seat navigator to find it.

Malcolm had been content to ride in the back. He was noticeably quiet during most of the two-hour drive. Every time I glanced in the rearview mirror, he had his earbuds in. I suspected he was nervous about meeting Aaron.

After talking at length with Malcolm the night before, I'd come to the conclusion that he was a polite young man, but shy and introverted—which could be misconstrued as surly.

I'd felt bad about our first meeting and apologized to him for how I behaved. "You must have thought I was the meanest mother on the planet," I said when we picked him up at the park.

He laughed at that. "Not even close."

When at last we turned onto the wooded lane that led to Aaron's house, I looked in the rearview mirror again and said to Malcolm, "We're here."

He pulled his earbuds out, turned off his music and gazed out the window at the hazy beams of sunlight shining into the otherwise shady green forest.

Though it was early summer, the blooms were out in full color. I pulled to a stop in the yard, removed my sunglasses and leaned forward over the steering wheel to peruse the property, which was located on the banks of a large, private lake.

The house was rustic-looking with pale gray cedar shakes and white trim. The yard had been lovingly landscaped with a wide green lawn that appeared freshly cut, classic evergreen shrubs, plenty of colorful flowers and a screened-in gazebo.

I opened the door and got out. A tremendous and unexpected feeling of joy flowed through me at the peacefulness—except of course for the sounds of the birds chirping and the insects buzzing in the trees.

The screen door on the house opened and slammed shut. Aaron was coming to greet us.

My whole body came alive with a zap of electricity at the sight of him, so different from how he'd looked when we last parted.

He appeared strong, healthy and robust, and there was color in his cheeks. He'd gained back the weight he'd lost during his time on the island, but still looked slender and fit. I could barely think or move as he crossed the lawn toward us, approaching with a smile and a wave.

Kaleigh was the first to run toward him and throw her arms around his waist. I was shocked by this—that she would feel so at ease with him.

"I can't believe it's really you!" she said. "You don't look the same at all!"

"I certainly *feel* better," he cheerfully replied, never taking his eyes off mine.

Those penetrating, smiling blue eyes...They still knocked me over, just like before.

No. Even more so now.

"Hi Aaron," I said warmly, and walked toward him.

Kaleigh stepped aside and I wrapped my arms around his shoulders, felt him take me by the waist and pull me close. His lips touched my neck and he whispered in my ear, "It's so good to see you."

"You, too," I replied as I forced myself to draw back and look him in the eye, so that I could introduce him to someone else.

"This is Malcolm," I said.

Malcolm, dressed in his usual Gothic black ensemble, with lip ring and tattoo on fine display, strode forward reservedly.

"Malcolm, this is Aaron Cameron," I added.

They shook hands.

"It's nice to meet you, Malcolm," Aaron said. "Do you all want to come inside? I don't know if you're hungry. I was thinking of boiling some mussels."

"I love mussels," Kaleigh replied, and we followed Aaron into the house.

⁓

The interior was cozy and cottagey, like something out of a dream, with large French windows overlooking the lake, and floor-to-ceiling bookcases along the far wall. Soft upholstered sofas and chairs sat on a wide plank floor of aged pine, with plenty of nicks and stress marks under our feet.

"It's so peaceful," I said, moving closer to the windows to look out. There was a small wharf with a shed and a single Adirondack chair facing the water. "Do you fish?"

"All the time," he replied. "It's funny, I was so sick of eating fish on the island. I thought if I ever made it home, I'd never eat fish again, but now I crave it. And I can't seem to go more than a few days without casting a line."

"Looks like they're jumping," I said, pointing to the circular ripples on the water.

"They're catching insects." He moved to the kitchen area and dumped a bowl of live mussels into a large pot on the stove.

"Malcolm, do you like to fish?" Aaron asked.

I turned to see Malcolm perusing the bookshelves, and was eager, myself, to go and see what Aaron liked to read.

Malcolm turned. "I don't know. I've never tried it."

"We could give it a go today if you want?" Aaron replied. "Sometimes I sit out on the dock, but I have the best luck when I take the rowboat out to the center of the lake where it's deep."

"I've never been in a rowboat before either," Malcolm quietly said, then he spotted Aaron's guitar on a stand in the corner of the room and approached it. "Do you play?" he asked with interest.

"Yes," Aaron replied, moving toward him. "I used to give lessons, but now I just play for fun."

Malcolm squatted down before the guitar to look at it more closely. "It's a Gibson J-29. That's a fine instrument."

"I just bought it last month," Aaron replied, "because I had to get everything new after being presumed dead. You can give it a try if you like."

"Maybe later." Malcolm rose to his feet.

Meanwhile, Kaleigh had plunked herself down on the sofa and was examining a brain teaser on the coffee table.

As I watched Aaron return to the kitchen and set a stack of four plates on the counter, I marveled at the fact that this situation could have been dreadfully awkward, but everything seemed effortless and relaxed. I didn't know what it was about Aaron Cameron that made everyone feel so at ease. He must be a fantastic therapist, I thought.

"Can I do anything to help?" I asked, strolling into the kitchen.

"Sure. Why don't we get the kids to help us take everything out to the gazebo? There's a picnic table out there. It's screened in, no bugs. These mussels will only take a few minutes to open up. Would you like a glass of wine?"

"I'd love one."

He opened the fridge and withdrew a bottle of white and opened it with a cork screw. Then he poured us each a glass and said to Kaleigh and Malcolm: "Why don't you two make yourselves useful and carry the plates and bread outside?"

Kaleigh leaped off the sofa to help, while Malcolm sauntered over casually.

"Do you like to swim?" Kaleigh asked Malcolm as she backed out the door.

"Yeah," he replied, following with the cutlery. "Especially when it's hot."

"I wonder if it's deep enough to jump off the dock," she added.

As soon as they left the house, I turned to Aaron. "I hope this is okay," I said. "I wasn't sure how to handle it."

"You handled it perfectly," he said. "Let's just have a nice time. Maybe I'll take him out in the boat later."

"So you can talk, and figure out how to handle things from here?" I added, and he nodded at me.

We had a nice time in the gazebo eating mussels and dipping bread in the creamy broth. Malcolm was curious about Aaron's experiences on the island, and Aaron regaled us with tales of the plane crash and stories of how he caught hares and lit fires without matches.

Malcolm was utterly fascinated and I was pleased to see how they interacted with each other, without awkwardness or resentment.

There were moments, however, when I found myself thinking of what the nurse had told me about Aaron's first night in the hospital when he'd become agitated and had required a sedative. I wondered how he was coping since his return to normal life. He seemed fine, but I wasn't sure if some of that was just for show. Or maybe he really was fully recovered, now that he was home again and living in a spot like this.

After we polished off the mussels, Malcolm and Kaleigh went outside to explore the yard and dock. The gazebo door swung shut behind them, and Aaron and I found ourselves sitting alone with the bottle of wine between us.

He poured me a second glass and refilled his own.

"I don't know how I can ever thank you," he said as he leaned forward over the table, regarding me intently. "Sometimes I wonder if you're some kind of angel from heaven. I feel like you keep saving me."

I shook my head. "You saved yourself on that island. How are you coping, by the way?"

He took a deep breath and let it out. "I still have nightmares sometimes, and occasionally I can get a bit emotional, but I'm working through it. Each day is better than the last, and *this* particular day...This is the best by far."

I smiled. "Well, the fact that we found Malcolm..." I shook my head in disbelief. "It's crazy, isn't it? Maybe there is some element of fate at work here. What are the odds that Kaleigh would end up in a guitar class with your son? And that they would figure out the connection?"

"How *did* they figure it out?" he asked.

I sighed heavily. "It's a long story and I'm not even sure where to begin." I reached for a piece of bread and tugged it apart with my fingers. "I can't lie. He had a rough childhood, Aaron, and from what I understand his mother never told him the truth about you, not until she saw news about the plane crash over a year ago. That's when she told Malcolm that his father had been killed in the crash. Kaleigh happened to ask him what happened to his dad, and when he told her about that, she immediately put two and two together. I should also mention that she had a bit of a crush on Malcolm. That's why they got to talking about personal stuff."

Aaron frowned. "She's only thirteen."

I ran a hand through my hair. "I know, and believe me, I wasn't happy about it when I found out, but I think it's okay now. He didn't even know how old she was because she lied about that. When he found out, he was pretty angry with her."

"I'm glad," Aaron replied, still frowning with concern as he turned to look out the screened windows. Malcolm and Kaleigh were skipping stones on the pebbly beach. "I'll talk to him," he said.

"Don't make a big deal about it," I replied. "I don't want him to feel like he screwed everything up. It wasn't his fault, it was Kaleigh's, and he hasn't had much luck in life so far."

"Him and me, both." Aaron turned to face me again and took another sip of wine. A small breeze blew a part in his brown hair and I felt a funny little sensation in my belly at how handsome he looked.

"So are you still seeing What's-His-Name?" Aaron asked.

"Josh?" I replied with a chuckle. "Yes."

Aaron bowed his head. "I hope he's a good guy. No wait…No I don't." His eyes lifted and he gave me a heated look. "I'd prefer it if he was an ass, if you really must know."

I laughed and raised an eyebrow. "Are you flirting with me, Dr. Cameron?"

He recognized the question as a replay from a moment we'd shared many months ago, but this time he answered differently.

"Yes, I am, Ms. Matthews. And it's a good thing Officer Josh isn't here. He might slap a set of cuffs on me."

I took another bite of bread. "So you know he's a cop. Did I tell you that before?"

"No, but I did a little research on my own. Kaleigh's on Twitter you know. She posts hints about things every once in a while. You're following her I hope."

"Of course. And you are as well?"

"Yeah, I couldn't help it. I wanted to stay in touch with the two of you somehow, but I didn't want to come off like a stalker."

"So you followed my daughter on Twitter? That's not stalker-ish at all."

We shared a laugh and sipped some more wine.

Aaron slowly spun his wineglass around by the stem. "Can I ask...?" He hesitated a moment, then gazed at me with interest. "Is it serious between you and this illustrious law enforcement officer?"

Feeling warm all of a sudden, I shrugged out of my white sweater, folded it and set it on the picnic table bench beside me.

"I'm supposed to have dinner with him tonight," I replied. "I think he might want to propose."

Something flashed in Aaron's eyes, then his shoulders rose and fell with a deep intake of breath. "Damn," he softly said. "Will you say yes?"

I felt no desire to be cryptic. "I don't know. I'm not positive he's the one." I gazed out at the lake. "You'd think it would be easier to know these things. Especially the second time around."

"If you have doubts," Aaron said, "you shouldn't rush into anything."

"That's what I think, but there are a lot of women out there—good friends of mine—who think I'd be a total nut to say no."

"It doesn't matter what anyone else thinks," Aaron said. "You're the only one whose opinion matters in this."

"Thank you, doctor. I appreciate the vote of confidence. I need to remember that there are choices. The sun won't rise and fall forever on this one decision. It will rise again tomorrow, just like it always does, regardless."

I felt caught suddenly in the striking color of his eyes and couldn't help but admire the broad cut of his shoulders in the shaded light of the gazebo. His masculine appeal caused a commotion in me.

He stared at me for a long while and I felt completely beguiled. I should have looked away, but I couldn't bring myself to leave the spell I was under. It was like some kind of drug.

The door to the gazebo swung open just then and Kaleigh peeked her head in to ask a question. "Can we go fishing off the dock?"

Aaron grinned at me as if to say we'd continue this later, then he rose from his place at the table.

"Sure. How about you guys help us clear away the mess? Then I'll get out the rods."

"You'll have to show us how," she said, moving to gather up the plates. "Neither of us has ever fished before."

"No problem," he replied. "It's not hard. You'll love it."

Malcolm came in to help as well, but it took me a moment to reboot my brain before I could join them.

⌒

When no one experienced even the smallest nibble after about twenty minutes, and the idea was presented that the rowboat should be launched, Kaleigh and I offered to remain on shore while the men rowed out to the center of the lake where the fish were jumping.

I was proud of Kaleigh for understanding that Aaron and Malcolm needed time alone to talk.

Before long, the mosquitoes appeared, so we decided to wait inside the house and watch from the windows.

I found Aaron's coffeemaker and filters and started a pot, then wrestled Kaleigh into helping me do the dishes.

Every few minutes I checked out the window to see how the men were doing. They were still fishing. I hoped Aaron had bug spray in his tackle box.

After we finished tidying the kitchen, Kaleigh sat down on the sofa to attempt the brain teaser game again, while I poured myself a cup of coffee and watched her. When at last she solved the puzzle, I decided to give it a try, so she got up to go and check out Aaron's books.

I was deeply focused on the game when I heard her call out to me. "Mom, look what I found."

"Hold on a second," I said, moving a piece of the puzzle from one spot to another.

"No, you have to look," she said. "It's Dad's journal."

My eyes lifted and everything seemed to happen in slow motion as she stood in front of the bookshelves, opening it to the first page.

"That's private." I rose to my feet. "You shouldn't look at it."
She didn't appear to have heard me. She was too deeply
engrossed in what she was reading.

"Kaleigh," I repeated. "Put it away. It's private."

"Wow," she said, still not hearing me at all. "Mom, you have
to read this."

"No," I said, crossing the room and snatching it out of her
grasp. "I'm not going to read it and neither should you. How
would you feel if someone read *your* diary?"

She looked up at me in shock. "I didn't think of it that way."

"Well, that's the way it is. This is Aaron's private journal. He
was very generous to share certain parts of it with us, and it was
nice of him today to tell us all those stories in the gazebo, but we
shouldn't read this."

Her eyes were wide. She looked pale.

"What's the matter?" I asked. "You look like you saw a ghost."

She shook her head. "Not a ghost. It was something else."

I wish I could say I told her to keep it to herself, but the temp-
tation was too great. I was entranced by everything to do with
Aaron, and to be presented with something he had written while
stranded on the island was too much for me to resist. "What was
it?"

Kaleigh stared at me uncertainly for several seconds, as if she wasn't quite sure if she should tell me. Then she glanced down at the book in my hands. "The stuff that's written on top of Dad's entries...Those are love letters," she finally confessed.

I frowned and looked down at the book. "What do you mean?"

My blood began to race.

"They're all written to you."

A half hour later, I'd read what I could decipher from the vertical writings that crisscrossed over the horizontal lines. At first it was mostly a record of the events that had occurred, similar to the entries written by Seth that Aaron had transcribed and sent to Gladys.

Towards the end, however, there were no further entries about what Aaron caught for dinner, or how he ran from a bear. Every page was a promise—always something specific and concrete—like a vow to take me to a particular movie or cook me a special dinner, and never to disappoint me.

The last thing I read, he had promised to buy me the house I wanted by the lake, with purple flowers.

Eventually I realized that Kaleigh was sitting beside me on the sofa with her hand on my back, asking, "Are you okay, Mom?"

I stood up and walked to the window, and looked down at the flower boxes full of purple and violet petunias.

The screen door opened suddenly and I could barely see straight through my blurry wet eyes. Holding the journal in my hands, I turned to face Aaron.

He stopped just inside the door, fishing rod in one hand, bucket of fish in the other, and all the color drained from his face.

"You weren't supposed to see that," he said.

Stomach churning, I set it down on the window sill. "I'm so sorry. I didn't mean to."

"Did you read it?"

Unable to lie to him, I nodded.

His Adam's apple bobbed and he bent forward to set down the bucket of fish and lean the rod up against the wall.

The door swung open and Malcolm followed him in. "Did you guys see what we caught?" he asked. "They were biting like crazy!"

"You had a good time?" I asked, not wanting to spoil what had been a perfect day for Malcolm.

Aaron wouldn't look at me. He noticed the full coffee pot and went to pour himself a cup.

Kaleigh immediately went to check out the fish in the bucket. "Wow," she said. "Let's go outside and take some pictures of them."

"Good idea," Malcolm replied.

Again, I was amazed by my young daughter's awareness and discretion.

As soon as the door swung shut behind them, I moved into the kitchen where Aaron was standing at the coffeemaker, looking down at the cup he'd just poured. I laid my hand on his shoulder.

"I'm sorry," I said. "I couldn't help it. I wanted to know what happened to you."

"I've told you what happened," he said, meeting my eyes. "How much did you read?"

"I read the letters you wrote," I replied.

He bowed his head and shook it. "I don't know what to say. I didn't want you to see those. I was half out of my mind, Carla."

"No..." I softly said.

He turned to me. "*Yes*. All I did those last few months was imagine that I was married to you and that you were waiting for me to come home to you. And I think I actually believed it when I built that raft and sailed for the shipping lanes. What sane man would do something like that?" He pinched the bridge of his nose. "What you read...It was fantasy. Maybe on a conscious level, but maybe not. I don't know." He brushed past me and moved to the window to retrieve the journal. "You won't need a restraining order or anything. I promise, I'm fine now."

A deep sorrow filled me, and I followed him to the window. "The purple flowers..." I said, looking out at the window box below us. "Were these for me?"

"No," he gently said. "They were for *me*, because by the end of it, that dream of yours was mine, too. When I saw this place for sale online, I couldn't believe what I was looking at. It was all here, the lake, the gazebo, even the flowers. I bought it, just as it was. I didn't plant a thing."

I looked out at the water. "But it's so perfect."

"I know."

We stood in silence, listening to Kaleigh and Malcolm laughing and talking outside.

"It's still my dream," I said. "And I'm not sorry I read those letters, Aaron. It was the most romantic thing I've ever seen. I'm only sorry I didn't ask your permission first. I feel like I stole something from you."

I felt his hand clasp mine. "No."

Then he took me into his arms and held me close.

"I'm the one who wants to steal something," he whispered in my ear. "And from a cop no less."

My breath hitched in my throat, and my pulse skyrocketed. "I'd really like it if you'd kiss me right now."

He drew back and took my face in his hands. Anticipation rose up from my depths, on top of the strange, unbreakable connection that seemed to form an electric current between us every time we met. Thoughts of him over the past few months, endless dreams of the two of us together, had dominated my world and filled me with doubts about my future. But all the doubt was fading away now. I knew what I wanted and I finally understood what it all meant—or maybe I always had. It wasn't until this moment that I became brave enough to trust it.

The sunlight beaming in the window reflected in Aaron's eyes. Then he pressed his lips lightly to mine.

I closed my eyes and relished the taste of him, the feel of his warm callused hands sliding down to the tops of my shoulders, then pulling my body close, anchoring me to him.

The kiss was hot and wet and filled me with inconceivable desire.

"Carla," he whispered in my ear, sending shivers straight down to my toes. "Don't leave. Don't go to him tonight. Stay here with me."

Without answering the question, I wrapped my arms around his neck, rose up on my toes and kissed him again, parting my lips and tasting the delicious flavor of his mouth.

My body felt charged and alive, and I wanted him with something close to an obsession. A feeling of profound joy and intimacy flowed through me, and I drew back to hold his face in my hands.

The door opened just then and we stepped apart.

Kaleigh and Malcolm walked in. "Are you going to show us how to gut them?" she asked, and I couldn't help but laugh at the ultimate shattering of the most romantic moment of my life.

"Sure," Aaron said, his eyes glistening with joy as he turned around. "And I hope you'll all stay for dinner because we caught enough to feed an army." He turned back to look at me again. "Unless you have other plans."

I gazed up at him with wonder. "No," I breathlessly replied, feeling a sense of completeness I'd never known before. "I don't have any other plans. We'd love to stay. Malcolm, you'll have to call your mom and let her know."

"Sure," he replied, and walked outside to dial her number.

Aaron reached for my hand and smiled. "Then let's go clean some fish."

Epilogue

Aaron

My story is not common, and today I look back on my life with immense gratitude for all that I've experienced, both the pleasures and the ordeals. I am a better man because of all of it, and my world is far richer than it was before.

Of course I am not speaking of material things. For a full year I learned to live without any of that. All I had was the great and astonishing magic of the universe, the company of the animals in the forest, a few tools and gifts from Seth, and the command of my intellect and imagination. But that's when I discovered the ultimate strength within me. No matter how dark things became, no matter how desperate or lonely, I always believed there was a light somewhere beyond my ability to see.

Even if you can't see it today, it might appear for you tomorrow.

What provided that light for me—when I sank very low and came close to giving up—was love.

I wasn't consciously aware at the time, but my love for Carla and the son I didn't know I had is what kept me going—though perhaps I did know. Maybe I always sensed Malcolm's presence in this world, and that's what I was praying for when the plane crashed into the wilderness: to be reunited with him.

I still don't know if it was God who answered my prayers. How can a man of science ever be certain of such spiritual things?

But there were many moments on the island when I felt an intense need to pray, even when I didn't think He was listening.

Now here I am with all my prayers answered. Is it possible He delivered my prayers to Carla, like whispers on a breeze? She often says she felt me, the promise of me, sometimes, even before she knew I existed.

We're married now, Carla and I. Of course, there were a few hurdles to clear before we could pledge our vows. She had to end things with Josh, and I had to confront Meg about our son and establish my rights as a father.

I asked her why she never told me about him. She admitted she didn't know if Malcolm was mine, and it was shame and remorse that drove her to the life she felt she deserved.

A DNA test has since proved my paternity. Meg has sought treatment for her addictions and is in our prayers every day.

I am pleased to report that Malcolm has become an important part of our lives. He's currently enrolled in a university music program while minoring in psychology. I am immensely proud of how far he's come and what he's accomplished.

Kaleigh is in high school now and plays guitar with me every day. She intends to pursue a career in nursing. She also has a boyfriend, which presents challenges at times, but he's a decent kid who treats her well. Carla and I often wonder whether or not they'll still be together five years from now.

In any case, it's Kaleigh's life and she will live it her own way. All we want is for her to be happy and do what she loves.

It's not always easy when you're young—to know what that is—but with experience comes wisdom, and in time all the puzzle pieces slide into place. Eventually, you know what you are meant for, and you can see clearly what will give your life meaning.

My life is no longer a puzzle. I understand my purpose and my joys.

Do you understand yours?

What a blessing life is. If you don't believe it, get up and watch the sunrise tomorrow or take time to gaze up at the stars. Listen to the restful sound of a mourning dove in the quiet woods, or the wind whispering through the leaves above you.

Contemplate all that you are grateful for, and never give up on your dreams. Most importantly, give your whole heart to all that you love in this life.

Questions for Discussion

1. In the first half of the novel, Carla and Aaron have not met. Do you believe that they were connected somehow? Discuss ideas and references that support your opinion.

2. How did you feel about Seth during his time as the protagonist of the novel? Was he likeable? Did you perceive him as heroic? Why or why not?

3. Do you believe Carla made a mistake when she married Seth? Why or why not?

4. In chapter forty-three when Carla believes Seth is alive, she asks: "Is it my duty to stay with him?" If it truly had been Seth who was found on the iceberg, what do you believe would have been the right thing for her to do?

5. Compare and contrast the differences between Carla's relationship with Aaron, both before and after meeting him in the hospital, and her relationship with Josh.

6. Do you believe Carla was right or wrong about putting her wedding ring back on before flying to Newfoundland to visit Seth? What would you have done in those circumstances?

7. How do you feel about the novel's conclusion? Was it realistic that Carla would be so ready to leave Josh behind after spending only a few days with Aaron? Would you have preferred to see it play out differently? How?

OTHER BOOKS IN THE COLOR OF HEAVEN SERIES

The COLOR *of* HEAVEN

A deeply emotional tale about Sophie Duncan, a successful columnist whose world falls apart after her daughter's unexpected illness and her husband's shocking affair. When it seems nothing else could possibly go wrong, her car skids off an icy road and plunges into a frozen lake. There, in the cold dark depths of the water, a profound and extraordinary experience unlocks the surprising secrets from Sophie's past, and teaches her what it means to truly live…and love.

Full of surprising twists and turns and a near-death experience that will leave you breathless, this story is not to be missed.

"A gripping, emotional tale you'll want to read in one sitting."
        —*New York Times* bestselling author, Julia London

"Brilliantly poignant mainstream tale."
        —4½ starred review, *Romantic Times*

The COLOR of DESTINY

Eighteen years ago a teenage pregnancy changed Kate Worthington's life forever. Faced with many difficult decisions, she chose to follow her heart and embrace an uncertain future with the father of her baby – her devoted first love.

At the same time, in another part of the world, sixteen-year-old Ryan Hamilton makes his own share of mistakes, but learns important lessons along the way. Twenty years later, Kate's and Ryan's paths cross in a way they could never expect, which makes them question the possibility of destiny. Even when all seems hopeless, could it be that everything happens for a reason, and we end up exactly where we are meant to be?

The COLOR *of* HOPE

Diana Moore has led a charmed life. She is the daughter of a wealthy senator and lives a glamorous city life, confident that her handsome live-in boyfriend Rick is about to propose. But everything is turned upside down when she learns of a mysterious woman who works nearby – a woman who is her identical mirror image.

Diana is compelled to discover the truth about this woman's identity, but the truth leads her down a path of secrets, betrayals, and shocking discoveries about her past. These discoveries follow her like a shadow.

Then she meets Dr. Jacob Peterson—a brilliant cardiac surgeon with an uncanny ability to heal those who are broken. With his help, Diana embarks upon a journey to restore her belief in the human spirit, and recover a sense of hope - that happiness, and love, may still be within reach for those willing to believe in second chances.

The COLOR of
A DREAM

Nadia Carmichael has had a lifelong run of bad luck. It begins on the day she is born, when she is separated from her identical twin sister and put up for adoption. Twenty-seven years later, not long after she is finally reunited with her twin and is expecting her first child, Nadia falls victim to a mysterious virus and requires a heart transplant.

Now recovering from the surgery with a new heart, Nadia is haunted by a recurring dream that sets her on a path to discover the identity of her donor. Her efforts are thwarted, however, when the father of her baby returns to sue for custody of their child. It's not until Nadia learns of his estranged brother Jesse that she begins to explore the true nature of her dreams, and discover what her new heart truly needs and desires…

The COLOR of A MEMORY

Audrey Fitzgerald believed she was married to the perfect man - a heroic firefighter who saved lives, even beyond his own death. But a year later she meets a mysterious woman who has some unexplained connection to her husband....

Soon Audrey discovers that her husband was keeping secrets and she is compelled to dig into his past. Little does she know... this journey of self-discovery will lead her down a path to a new and different future - a future she never could have imagined.

Praise for Julianne MacLean's historical Romances

"MacLean's compelling writing turns this simple, classic love story into a richly emotional romance, and by combining engaging characters with a unique, vividly detailed setting, she has created an exceptional tale for readers who hunger for something a bit different in their historical romances."

—*BOOKLIST*

"You can always count on Julianne MacLean to deliver ravishing romance that will keep you turning pages until the wee hours of the morning."

—Teresa Medeiros

"Julianne MacLean's writing is smart, thrilling, and sizzles with sensuality."

—Elizabeth Hoyt

"Scottish romance at its finest, with characters to cheer for, a lush love story, and rousing adventure. I was captivated from the very first page. When it comes to exciting Highland romance, Julianne MacLean delivers."

—Laura Lee Guhrke

"She is just an all-around wonderful writer, and I look forward to reading everything she writes."

—Romance Junkies

About the Author

Julianne MacLean is a USA Today bestselling author of many historical romances, including The Highlander Series with St. Martin's Press and her popular American Heiress Series with Avon/Harper Collins. She also writes contemporary mainstream fiction, and The Color of Heaven was a USA Today bestseller. She is a three-time RITA finalist, and has won numerous awards, including the Booksellers' Best Award, the Book Buyer's Best Award, and a Reviewers' Choice Award from Romantic Times for Best Regency Historical of 2005. She lives in Nova Scotia with her husband and daughter, and is a dedicated member of Romance Writers of Atlantic Canada. Please visit Julianne's website for more information and to subscribe to her mailing list to stay informed about upcoming releases.

OTHER BOOKS BY
JULIANNE MacLean

The American Heiress Series:
To Marry the Duke
An Affair Most Wicked
My Own Private Hero
Love According to Lily
Portrait of a Lover
Surrender to a Scoundrel

The Pembroke Palace Series:
In My Wildest Fantasies
The Mistress Diaries
When a Stranger Loves Me
Married By Midnight
A Kiss Before the Wedding - A Pembroke Palace Short Story
Seduced at Sunset

The Highlander Series:
Captured by the Highlander
Claimed by the Highlander
Seduced by the Highlander
The Rebel – A Highland Short Story

The Royal Trilogy:
Be My Prince
Princess in Love
The Prince's Bride

Harlequin Historical Romances:
Prairie Bride
The Marshal and Mrs. O'Malley
Adam's Promise

Time Travel Romance
Taken by the Cowboy

Contemporary Fiction:
The Color of Heaven
The Color of Destiny
The Color of Hope
The Color of a Dream
The Color of a Memory
The Color of Love
The Color of the Season
The Color of Joy